ANNA IN CHAINS

Other titles in the Library of Modern Jewish Literature

ANNA
IN CHAINS

MERRILL JOAN GERBER

SYRACUSE UNIVERSITY PRESS

First Edition 1998

98 99 00 01 02 03   6 5 4 3 2 1

The first eight stories in this book were previously published in *Chattering Man* (Longstreet Press, 1991). "The Leaf Lady" first appeared in *Crosscurrents*. "Mozart You Can't Give Them" and "Comes an Earthquake" first appeared in *The Sewanee Review*. "The Blood Pressure Bunch and the Alzheimer's Gang" first appeared in *Amelia*. "Starry Night" first appeared in *Phoebe: A SUNY Women's Studies Journal*. "Hear No Entreaties, Speak No Consolations" first appeared in *The Chattahoochee Review*. ∞™

The paper used in this publication meets the minimum requirements of American National Standard for Information Sciences—Permanence of Paper for Printed Library Materials, ANSI Z39.48-1984.

Library of Congress Cataloging-in-Publication Data

Gerber, Merrill Joan.
    Anna in chains / Merrill Joan Gerber. — 1st ed.
       p.   cm. — (The Library of modern Jewish literature)
    ISBN 0-8156-0484-X (alk. paper)
      1. Aged women—California—Los Angeles—Fiction. 2. Jewish women—California—Los Angeles—Fiction. I. Title. II. Series.
    PS3557.E664A84   1997
    813'.54—dc21   97-29662

Manufactured in the United States of America

For
Cynthia Ozick

CONTENTS

ANNA IN CHAINS

"RAD, MAN"

On the TV screen some thug with long blond hair named Hulk Hogan was wrestling some other hooligan wearing leopard-skin jockey shorts. Their grunts, as they hit the floor, sounded to Anna like a hippopotamus in labor.

Anna's grandsons, Abram and David, leaned forward on the couch, staring at the screen without blinking—two complete morons. At each sound of a human head hitting the canvas, a burst of unintelligible speech came out of Abram's mouth and his bare, tanned knees came up as if he were having a fit. (Despite the fact that it was December, he was wearing some garish flowered shorts that had cost Carol thirty dollars.) He leaned over suddenly and punched his brother who cried out, "Rad, man! Rad!" Then the two boys proceeded to punch each other violently for about twenty seconds.

Carol was calmly reading the paper and drinking her coffee at the table. Either she was deaf, or dead, to ignore the carnage taking place here. How could her daughter, how could *anyone*, live like this? These boys weren't civilized human beings. They were cave men just out of the bush. The sounds that came forth from these children's mouths were unbelievable (and not only from their mouths). Anna felt sorry for Carol, but what could she do? She was supposed to mind her own business no matter how bad things got around here.

She scrutinized her older grandson. He was just fifteen

and was six feet three inches tall. His good looks were no fault of his. Plus he was adopted, and God only knew what else would turn up in him. He held in his lap a soup bowl piled with eight scoops of Heavenly Hash ice cream and raised to dangerous heights with swirls of fake whipped cream shot from a can. Anna had noticed that he'd emptied into his dish the entire ice cream carton and the entire can of whipped cream which her daughter had just bought yesterday at the supermarket. He'd only stopped his frantic squirting from the nozzle when the last blurps had spat dots of cream all over himself and the couch. And this was right after he'd eaten a gigantic dinner—three burritos with red sauce (whatever was in them Anna should never know from it). The food in this house didn't last twenty-four hours after Carol dragged in two hundred dollars' worth from the car, bag after heavy bag. And did the boys help her carry in the groceries? No, they were too busy watching TV. "Later! I'll do it *later!*" was their refrain—a reflex wailed constantly, whether or not anyone was asking them to do anything. ("Goodnight," Anna would say, and they'd yell, "I'll do it later!")

Anna had addressed them many times (both in and out of their mother's presence) in the two weeks she'd been recuperating here. She had told them, speaking very slowly, in a way that even a total retard could understand, that they only had one mother in this life and she was the only one they were ever going to get and they had better treat her with respect. She wasn't going to last forever and at the rate they were wearing her out she wasn't even going to last another week. *Especially* with no father around to keep them in line. By the way their eyes went blank, Anna knew she should have saved her energy. It all went in one ear and right out the other. As for Carol, if she were listening to Anna give her speech, her eyes got small and hard in a way that made Anna's heart skip a few beats. But she wasn't going to be intimidated. She had her piece to say and she was going to say it; maybe it wouldn't sink in till ten years from now, and maybe never, but at least she could feel she'd done her part.

Now Abram stopped gobbling ice cream long enough to pull off his shoes and socks and toss them at Mr. T, the dog. Between the smells that came from both ends of the animal, and those that came from Abram's feet, it was no wonder Anna couldn't eat here, was nauseated all the time. The instant she got better from her fall, she would be out of here and back to her own apartment like a shot. In fact, as soon as she got home to LA, she planned to start a lawsuit against the high school where she went to her night classes—whose pothole she had fallen in and thereby broken her foot. She couldn't *wait* to get home. God save her from the day she would ever have to live with either of her two children—this arrangement was no good and what's more it could only get worse.

"Time to light the Chanukah candles," Carol announced from the table. "Also time to rewind the movie, boys, because we have to return the tape to Leo's before nine."

"This is a *rented* movie?" Anna asked her daughter. "I thought this was just regular TV junk."

"It's only ninety-nine cents to rent a movie on a weeknight, Mom," Carol said. "It's no big deal."

"Why is it that everything they do has to cost money? Didn't they ever hear of reading a book?"

"They can't learn everything from books," Carol said. "They get plenty of that in school."

"They can learn something from baseball cards?"

"Yeah," Abram interrupted, "especially from baseball cards. Hey, Mom—I need money for another pack. You promised. Brian got Peewee Reese, the lucky dog."

"I know exactly what they learn from TV," Anna said. "They learn how to murder drug pushers and how to throw someone out a window. But what talents do they get from baseball cards?"

"Well, for one thing," Carol said, "they trade and sell them. They learn about the realities of the market place."

"Reality! This is reality? VCRs, video games, new bicycles, new skateboards—they think it all comes to them at the snap of a finger."

"My children know more about reality, Mom," Carol said coldly, "than anyone their age should ever know." Anna knew exactly to what Carol was referring; her daughter was going to use that as an excuse to spoil her sons for the rest of their lives.

"Rad!" breathed Abram toward the TV screen. The gorilla in the jockey shorts was now spinning the blond guy over his head like a helicopter's blades. Anna closed her eyes till the thump occurred and only opened them when she was sure the body had hit down. Abram swung his long arm forward and hit a button on the VCR. The screen began to flutter and show the wrestlers doing everything backwards. They rose up from the floor like ballerinas.

In actual fact Anna was not against Carol's spending money on the boys for cultural purposes—music lessons would have been fine, even *English* lessons! But Hebrew lessons? That was going too far. The way the kids fought Carol, who literally had to force them into the car twice a week to go to *shul*, was a disgrace. Why was she wasting her time? Did she think these hoodlums of hers were going to turn into little rabbis? Again, on this issue, Anna had plenty to say, but maybe this wasn't the right moment.

"Now let's do the candles," Carol said firmly. "Then we'll go to Leo's."

"I don't want to go," David said. "I'm busy."

"I'll only go if you take me to Big Five first," Abram said. "I need new tennis shoes."

"Not tonight," Carol said. "You just got new tennis shoes."

"I didn't *just* get them. Besides, Mr. T chewed holes in them."

6

. . . . .

"That's because you throw him your shoes as if they're meat bones," Carol said. "Now—whose turn is it to light the candles?"

"His," both boys said, each pointing at his brother.

"All right, you do it tonight, David. I think Abram did it last night." Carol went to get the matches from a high shelf. As she reached for them, Anna saw how thin her arm was, how lank and frail she seemed. To handle boys like this, a person would need to have the strength of an ox. To do it all without a man to help—that was the real tragedy.

On the counter between the kitchen and the family room sat the menorah which had belonged to Anna's mother. It was made of tin. Her mother had paid five cents for it in 1910 in a grocery store in Brooklyn. Anna, having long since had enough of Jewish nonsense herself, had asked her daughters a few years ago which one wanted the family heirloom. She didn't have the heart to throw it out. It was so lightweight Carol had had to steady it on the counter with the end of one of Abram's small barbells. The tin was embossed with the image of a real menorah: brass—heavy and authentic. The tin cylinders which held the swirled, colored candles were deformed, pressed out of shape by time. Each night that the boys had been forced by their mother to light the candles, Anna had felt something close in her throat, some soundless gasp escape her. Her own Abram had been observant; he had lit the candles seriously, said the prayer. To whom? For what? What had his prayers got him but leukemia at fifty-five? And left her here, lost in this life without him, an intruder in her daughter's household, an extra person who belonged to no one.

"Where's the box of candles?" David demanded. He had a voice like a hog-caller. Words didn't exit his lips, they exploded forth. "I don't want two yellows next to each other. They look gross. Who put them in like that?"

"I did," Carol said.

"What are you, some kind of retard?" David accused her.

"Don't speak to your mother that way," Anna said.

"But she is," Abram defended his brother. "Mom's just out of it all the time. She's a total nerd."

This boy who was now addressing Anna and insulting his mother was the child who bore Anna's husband's name and *wasn't even from their genuine family*. She didn't believe in adoption and now she had doubts about personal childbirth as well. Even her other daughter's children—college girls now—were not always to her taste, to say the least. Their genes, of course, were diluted by the father. In every birth, unfortunately, there was always a father in the picture. In the case of her grandsons, she didn't know which boy was worse—the one related to her by blood or the one not. She decided she might take both boys out of her will as soon as she got home. David, who had the genes of her ancestors as well as hers and her husband's and Carol's, also carried the weird genes of his father, the madman who had killed himself with a vacuum hose and carbon monoxide from his car exhaust. No one Anna knew was acceptably related to her—not purely, not in a way she could tolerate. No one satisfied her but herself.

In a flood of indignation, she began to berate the boys despite Carol's warning look. "You children are hateful, disrespectful, rude, loud, and ungrateful." She hit them with her powerful vocabulary. "You are thoughtless, demanding, greedy, and inconsiderate." Then she added "Dirty." Then, "Filthy." Finally, directed at Abram, "Smelly."

Abram muttered something. Could Anna have heard right? With his handsome head bowed, could her grandson actually have said the unforgivable to her, *"Fuck off"*?

Anna thought she could possibly faint now that she had lived to see this day. She closed her eyes while the room spun. When she opened them, the Chanukah candles were lit, and Carol was reading from the side of the box the end of the prayer in English.

8

". . . Blessed art thou, O Lord our God, King of the
Universe, who has kept us in life, and hast preserved us,
and enabled us to reach this season . . ."

Preserved me too long, Anna thought. *Enough already.*

It was deadly quiet in the house. Carol had taken Abram
to return the video tape to Leo's, and David had gone off to
his bedroom and slammed the door. Only Mr. T and Anna
were on the couch. Mr. T had his nose in Anna's lap, and
she didn't have the strength to push him off. She already
could feel fleas creeping up her arm.

She sat in the dark, with only the glow from the Chanukah candles lighting the room. She could try to have
another talk with Carol when she came home, but what
point would there be? Carol always took the boys' side. She
had the same defense each time—"They've been deprived
of enough as it is, Mom. They've had a very hard time. And
they're no different from other kids their ages—thirteen
and fifteen are very hard times, they're adolescents, they
need to make noise, to release energy. They have very
strong forces to deal with, peer pressure, their sex
drives . . ."

"Don't fill me in with the details," Anna had said. "I
watch Dr. Ruth. I know all about it."

She sat there, absently patting Mr. T. His tail thumped.
At least with dogs, you could alter them, tone them down,
defuse their energies. Anna wished she could alter the
world, start over and give her daughter a good husband
who could earn a living and wasn't crazy and wouldn't kill
himself, give her two sons without anyone's genes at all, just
two perfect respectful children, give her good health and a
house out of the smog somewhere. And while she was at it,
she'd bring Abram back for herself, and they'd take a
condominium on the beach, also out of the smog.

Loud hammering came from David's room. What was he
doing now? Knocking holes in the wall? She didn't have the

. . . . .

strength to go down the hall to see, not with the heavy cast on her foot. But maybe she'd better. With his stupidity, who knew what he was capable of?

"What's going on?" Anna said, opening his door. She ignored a big sign that said, "KNOCK FIRST OR YOU'RE DEAD."

"Nothing," David said. He was hammering small wooden boards together on his desk.

"Don't tell me nothing when you're doing something. I'm not blind and I'm not deaf, not yet," Anna said.

"I'm making a bed."

"You don't have a bed?"

"It's for my wrestler," David said.

"For who?"

"Hulk Hogan."

"Oh," Anna said. She was silent.

"Want to see him?" His voice, for once, was not a bark.

"Maybe . . ." Anna said.

David flung himself over his bed and pulled from beneath it a shoe box. Inside, laid on tissue paper, covered with a folded wash cloth, *tucked in*, was a miniature rubber thug, Hulk Hogan, sleeping peacefully within the outlines of his huge, ugly muscles.

"Want to hold him?" David asked. He offered her the shoebox.

Anna stepped back. "Maybe later," she said. She was touched by the vision of the doll. To think that David was building a bed for that creature made her grandson seem human, even sweet.

She left David hammering and wandered down the hall. On Abram's door was the sign, "YOU'RE DEAD IF YOU EVEN TOUCH THE DOORKNOB. DON'T BOTHER TO KNOCK. *NO ONE* COMES IN HERE."

Anna pushed in the door. She expected the room to be a shambles, a pigpen. But when she turned on the light, she saw first the baseball cards, pinned in their plastic enve-

lopes in neat rows on the corkboard which lined one whole
wall. Then she saw the airplane models, hanging on strings
from the ceiling, silver fighter jets and brown vintage
bombers, wafting in the draft from the heater vent, Abram's
bed was made as tightly as a marine's. On his desk were a
notebook and an open volume of the encyclopedia; Abra-
ham Lincoln's face stared up at her from a photograph. It
was clear her grandson had been working on some kind of
report. Anna was having trouble breathing deeply. Not only
could Abram the hoodlum maybe read, but he could also
maybe write.

She carefully backed out of the room and closed the door. **11**
In the TV room Mr. T had started barking violently. He ran
from one end of the room to another, convulsed with hysterical yaps. David came out of his bedroom.

"I better go see what's up." His voice had suddenly become deep. "Someone might be in the yard." Boy and dog
went outside through the patio door, and Anna found her
way again to the couch, dragging her foot in its cast in the
hospital-issue Abominable Snowman slipper. She heard Mr.
T still yapping maniacally. David rushed inside and
grabbed one of the burning Chanukah candles from the
menorah, the one on top, the *shamesh*, and ran out again.
"I need to see over the fence," he yelled. "Something bad is
out there. Maybe a rat."

The next thing Anna saw through the plate glass window
was an explosion. A flash of fire like an atom bomb. Then:
David's screams.

She ran outside—she didn't know how she got there with
her broken foot—to find her grandson on fire: there he
was, huddled by the fence, a screaming flare of flame.

Don't, she commanded God. *Don't you dare do this.*

She found the hose, turned it on full, aimed it, tripped on
the dog, saw stars overhead in the sky, found her balance,
forced a Red Sea of water on his precious life. He was now
down in the dirt; he knew to roll around on the ground,

from television. She had seen him see that very scene on television on a murder mystery program. Thank God for television.

"Call 911! Call 911!" he yelled to Anna. That, too, from the movies. Last weekend Carol had rented *Down and Out in Beverly Hills*. Thank God for Hollywood. She pulled the wet child with her into the house and called 911.

When Carol and Abram came home, Anna and David were under a Charlie Brown quilt on the couch, watching a movie called *Pee Wee's Big Adventure*. David was in dry clothes and Anna was holding his hand; she was surprised at how huge it was, almost a man's hand. In the movie some daffy guy with a beanie on his head kept pedalling his bike backwards. David laughed everytime Pee Wee made a funny face, and when his body vibrated against Anna's chest, she laughed too.

"Should I tell them now?" David whispered into Anna's ear.

"Wait a few minutes. Let your mother get her breath." She touched David's face gently. His eyelashes had been singed off, but that was all. The paramedic had told Anna he would be fine. By some miracle, the Angel of Death had passed over the house like a silver jet.

But if it hadn't been Chanukah, David wouldn't have taken a candle out into the yard. If there hadn't been a can of charcoal lighter at the fence, he wouldn't have stood on it. If it hadn't tipped over, the cap wouldn't have come off. If the hot wax hadn't dripped down and ignited the charcoal lighter . . .

Well, never mind. If Anna had been born a Russian princess! If the world were square! If God were a kind man with a long beard!

Carol was busy in the kitchen unpacking bags of groceries. "I just stopped off to get a few more things we need," she called to her mother. Abram was standing by, yelling

. . . . .

"Neato" every time she unpacked an item that pleased him: a six-pack of Pepsi; frozen burritos; chocolate mint cream pie. When she pulled out bags of carrots, oranges, broccoli, he rolled his eyes and said, "Retch," accompanied by sound effects. Anna noticed that he was wearing new white tennis shoes after all. They had orange lightning bolts on them.

"Hey, David," Abram yelled into the dimness of the TV room. "Mom let me rent *Ghostbusters* again."

"Rad," David said, a little weakly. "Really rad."

"And we got another Heavenly Hash ice cream."

"Could we please have some over here before it's all gone?" Anna asked immediately. "With whipped cream if possible."

"Your wish is my command," Abram said. He danced around under the kitchen light like a boxer in his new shoes.

"But don't bring it to us yet. You help your mother unpack first," Anna said.

"And then we have something to tell you," David added. "It'll blow your mind."

THE LEAF LADY

The Leaf Lady was swirling her broom around on the cracked cement; no matter when Anna came up Granger Street, pulling her despised cart behind her, she saw the same angry woman, dressed in a blue bathrobe, jerking her yellow broom from side to side and daring the universe to dirty her sidewalk. Anna had no doubt that she was a landlady, probably as bad as her own.

A leaf came down. The Leaf Lady pounced, attacked it with a flurry of broomstraws, shunted it into her dustpan, delivered it triumphantly into her silver trash bag. Then she planted her feet apart, looked up, and waited for another to come down from the stunted, anemic tree.

Old ladies like this one gave a bad name to all old ladies. If Anna could be bumping along the street shaped like a beachchair or a candlestick or a rye bread, she would definitely prefer it to looking like this white-haired object in whose form she was housed. She glanced in the window of a car and winced at her reflection. Typical. The rounded shoulders, the delicate jowls, the fallen, sunken, loose skin of the face, the watery eyes. Even the ears on old people got huge, stretched out, as if to remind the world to speak up—more was needed, more of everything, if the old were to receive even a tiny bit of what used to be their due.

There was no point in trying to hide her age like some of the women at the Center did, with their platinum hairdos and their red-white-and-blue makeup. Besides, little things

gave them away. In one second their stooped backs and
their wire carts on wheels told the whole predictable story:
osteoporosis and a dead husband. An army of women like
Anna walked the streets. Who needed names or histories?
You could guess a hundred life-stories and be right ninety-
nine times: the one-room apartment, enough money in the
bank to make up what Social Security didn't pay for, the
big-shot children (at the Center, where Anna ate lunch
every day, "movie producer" was the favorite; doctors,
lawyers—they weren't so impressive any more).

16   Anna sighed with regret. In that department she was
sorely lacking—her youngest daughter, Carol, was the
widow of a lunatic who had killed himself (thank God, at
least, for that) and her oldest, Janet, was married to a
professor. Neither of her children was ever going to provide
Anna with the key to a fancy condominium with soundproof
walls. This was her heart's desire: to live in a place with no
Armenians, no Russians, no gays, no babies, no aspiring
musicians, no noises, no smells. And no landladies.

She dragged her cart down the curb and was nearly run
down by a Mexican speeding by in an ancient red truck.
And no Mexicans, she added. A warning flag flashed in her
mind. These conveniences she wished for she would find
soon enough in a hole in the ground. And for much cheaper
than in a condominium. She shouldn't wish for something
she wasn't ready for. Bernie, at the Center, warned everyone he met: "Don't have fancy wishes—God might make
them come true."

God was a subject she wasn't going to get into now. She
had to remember her shopping list. Although she wasn't
superstitious—she didn't go hopping right now over to some
tree to knock on wood that she had a good heart; she didn't
spit to ward off the Evil Eye—she said aloud for the record,
"For a hole in the ground I can wait a while."

She pulled her cart up the side of the far curb,
grudgingly grateful that she had crossed Santa Monica
Boulevard again and was still in one piece. Accidents were

the foe of old women. One day you were on your two feet, the next day you were in traction in a hospital room with some big-mouth who wouldn't shut up for five minutes.

Feeling she had crossed a wide, dangerous river, Anna glanced back across the street and saw the Leaf Lady watching her. She stared back. The old witch shook the top of her broom at her. She made shapes with her mouth. Anna guessed she was cursing and was not surprised. Everyone was crazy, and you couldn't make a friend in this world even if you wanted to.

In the Alpha Beta she got her coupons ready. Her fingers **17** trembled as she put the flimsy bits of newspaper in order. Twelve cents off on orange juice, twenty-five cents off on a dozen eggs, fifty cents off on a pound of bacon. Nevermind that her sister Gert was outraged by Anna's fondness for bacon; when the Messiah came down personally to Anna and gave her one good reason why Abram had died so young, and *apologized,* then maybe she would consider giving up bacon. In the meantime she would eat what she liked.

She hooked her cart to the wire edge of the store's shopping wagon and began to push. The rubber wheels jammed and the steel bar caught Anna just under her breasts. The air went out of her. She stopped to wait for the pain to recede, and, as she stood there, a wagon crashed into her ankles. She cried out and spun around. A woman wearing a purple turban and a flowered pantsuit said, "Honey, this is no place to stand around daydreaming. This is heavy traffic."

"You should watch where you're going!"

"And *you* should go back to Russia where you belong!" the woman said, brandishing an armful of gold bracelets at Anna.

Russia! To be mistaken for a foreigner when she had been born in America!

"Oh go to hell," Anna said.

She gave a push on her wagon and got herself into the aisle with coffee and tea. Now came the business of comparing prices. She wasn't going to let them take her for a fool. One brand of coffee was eighteen-and-a-half cents an ounce, another was twenty-two cents an ounce. She would be here all morning if she had to, making calculations, but it was necessary.

She never even drank a whole cup of coffee. She made it for the warmth, for the smell, for the way the steam penetrated the china cup and heated her fingers. She always put in sugar and cream and let the aroma warm her cold face in **18** the morning. She allowed herself this indulgence: to remember Abram every morning, the way he had enjoyed his breakfast, the two sunnyside-up eggs she fried for him, like happy eyes on his plate; how he wolfed down his toast, gulped his coffee. His appetites had been huge and wonderful.

She glanced up and thought she was having a stroke. Abram stood right next to her, as he would have looked if he'd grown old. He was in baggy gray pants, peering at boxes of teabags on the shelf next to the coffee. Oh—but he looked pathetic; his stretched-out brown sweater was pilled and stained, his shoes were scuffed and dusty, his wavy hair ragged. But he had the same hairline, the same bushy, down-slanted eyebrows, the crinkles around the good-natured eyes. Anna felt her heart skip and realized she had stopped breathing.

A miracle. Maybe she wouldn't buy bacon. She set her coupons down on the shelf and pretended to be examining a can of coffee. She glanced sideways at the man's shopping wagon. In it were six cans of Campbell's tomato soup. *God in heaven!* Like in her dream! In her dream, Abram was always in a shabby little room somewhere, without her, all alone, bent over his hot plate, heating up a can of tomato soup. There was a telephone in his room, an old black one, sitting like a squashed cross on a rickety wooden table. But

· · · · ·

in the dream she never knew the number, she could never reach him.

The man had Abram's large nose. He was shorter than Abram, but even men lose calcium, their spines shrink. All those years alone, twenty-three years alone in that room. What did he think about there? Her! He must think about Anna and the girls when they were little. Maybe even now, as he peered at the shelves in the Alpha Beta, he was thinking of her, the breakfasts she had made him, the pleasure she had given him. Tears flooded her eyes. *I'm all alone, too! I think of you every minute of my life!*

He selected Swee Touch Nee tea, the kind she always used, and she knew this was some kind of visitation. She reached out her hand, almost ready to pluck the sleeve of his sweater, to point herself out to him, but drew it back. The Anna he must remember was a young woman (only in her fifties!), whose face was still smooth, whose breasts (even then!) were like when she was sixteen. He was dreaming of his young wife; she was remembering her young husband, and here they stood, side-by-side, lives like pitchers that were tipped over and only a few drops left inside.

He took his tea and shuffled off behind his cart. Even the way his pants sank low on his hips was the same as Abram. But he was so shabby, so alone in the world, it broke her heart to see it. She made a sobbing sound and dug in her pocketbook for a handkerchief. She never carried on like this, but she had lost control. He was disappearing around the corner, going to the next aisle. She felt she had to hurry or he would be gone. She pushed hard against her cart, the wheels locked again, she was punched in the chest.

She sobbed openly as she struggled to push the wagon; it was like moving a mountain up the aisle. She turned the corner, knocking some bags of potato chips off a display. There he was! In front of frozen foods! Holding a pepperoni pizza in his hand, examining the pale, cheesy face of it.

. . . . .

Abram never ate a pizza in his life! Even when the girls
first tasted it in high school, when they wanted the family to
go out to dinner and eat it, he scorned it. Dough heavy as
lead, he used to say. With cheese and meat mixed together!
A horror, a disgusting invention.

Her senses returned to her. She let him go and turned her
wagon the other way. What did she want him for anyway—a
filthy old man who ate pizza, who now had an ugly frown on
his face?

Her list, her shopping list. She had been here all this time
and had bought nothing and was exhausted already. Her
chest ached, the backs of her ankles were scraped. And now
. . . now she had lost her coupons! They were gone, not in
her hand, not in her bag, not in her wagon. After she had
scrupulously cut them out of the paper this morning, not
one of them with a ragged edge so the checkout girl could
complain, accuse Anna of sloppiness.

She began to retrace her steps, looking on the floor for
her coupons. She wanted that fifty cents off on bacon. She
was going to go home and cook half a pound for her dinner
and eat it all at once, piece by piece, knowing it was from a
pig, making it clear to God that she knew.

She found no coupons on the floor of the Alpha Beta.
Anna walked slowly around the whole store, looking. She
was about to give up when she spied an empty wagon by the
bananas, just sitting there, abandoned. And in it were the
same three coupons she had lost: for eggs, for bacon, for
orange juice. The edges were ragged; someone less careful
than she had torn them out of the paper. Whoever owned
them must have got disgusted, as she often did. Couldn't
find the juice. Didn't want to bother. The wagon didn't
work and the person got fed up and walked out.

To test this assumption, Anna jiggled the wagon and felt
the heavy locking of its rubber wheels. There—it was like a
dead whale and it didn't happen just to her. But this person
had been smart and just walked out. If more people did
that, the Alpha Beta would wake up, oil their wheels.

20

She lifted the coupons out of the wagon and arranged
them in her hand. She felt lucky. At least she could salvage
something from this shopping trip. Maybe today would even
turn out to be her lucky day. Maybe she would buy a lottery
ticket when she checked out. What would she do with fifty
thousand dollars? Buy a Steinway Grand. Buy two. Her
spirits were beginning to revive.

"That's the woman!" a man yelled behind her just as she
was picking up a package of bacon. "She's the one!" The
old man, the Abram who wasn't Abram, was pointing his
finger at her, an inch from her nose, and the woman in the
purple turban and flowered pantsuit was running toward
her, her face like a tornado.

"Did you steal my coupons?" she screamed, while the old
man was blabbering, spit coming from his lips. "She took
them right out of your wagon, I saw her!"

Anna waved the tattered coupons in the air. "Here! Take
them! Who needs them? I thought someone left them there
. . . no one was by the wagon . . . I had my own coupons, I
brought them with me . . . I lost them."

"Yeah, yeah, yeah!" the woman said, tearing them from
Anna's fingers. "Thief! I should have them call the police on
you."

The old man, with his ugly, unfamiliar face, was glaring
at her. His eyes were vicious.

Go eat your pepperoni! Anna thought. *Go to hell, all of
you.*

She unhooked her little cart from the big wagon and
dragged it toward the front of the store. She started out the
IN door and it hit her in the face, opening automatically as
someone approached it from outside.

Blindly, she backed away and found the other door,
clattered out with her cart, crossed Santa Monica Boulevard. Cars honked and screeched around her. Let them run
her over, she'd thank them.

The Leaf Lady looked up as Anna clanked her empty cart
over the curb. She came to stand in the middle of the street,

her robe gaping open, holding her broomstick like a spear. She pointed it at Anna's empty cart. "What's the matter?" she said. "There's nothing good enough for you in the whole store?"

"Oh drop dead," Anna said. She was crying and couldn't see where she was going.

"I wouldn't do you the favor," the Leaf Lady said. "Believe me, not even if it was the end of the world."

"If it was the end of the world, we'd all be better off," Anna said, moving right along.

"Not me," the Leaf Lady called after her. "I got property all over Venice."

"So I own two pianos," Anna yelled over her shoulder. "And even so, I say we'd be better off!"

"The kind of music you must play, maybe you're right!"

But Anna wasn't going to answer such stupidity. She dragged her wagon homeward, watching out for potholes.

MOZART YOU
CAN'T GIVE THEM

In the downstairs apartment the young Mexican boy began to knock his head against the wall. Sometimes Anna thought it was just the low bass beat of some tenant's stereo, but as soon as she realized it wasn't regular, she knew it was the boy starting his morning tantrum. At least if he had some sense of rhythm—a little drummer boy. But he wasn't musical, only crazy. At almost the same instant the Russian lady across the courtyard began playing violent streaks of dissonance on her cello. Immediately Anna pictured a blackboard, wide and colorless as Russia, and across it came the shrieking chalk, an empty train scraping and grinding its way over the bleak plains. The woman should have stayed in Russia where there was more space, and not moved here to live ten feet from Anna and give her a headache every day.

As if all that weren't enough, Anna heard the clatter of the barbecue lid being lifted outside, and she rushed to lock her windows. On the tiny balcony next to Anna's, the father of the Armenian family was lighting the barbecue starter again. What was wrong with these people that they had to cook three times a day over charcoal? Didn't they know how to use a stove? If they were civil human beings in the first place, she would tell them that this kind of cooking could give them cancer. But when she slammed the sliding glass door shut, the man always sneered at her, looking like a walrus with his hanging mustache, and threw more lighter on the coals, for spite.

Charred edges of meat, which tasted like heaven itself, could kill you. What couldn't kill you? Pickled herring could kill you, lox could kill you, everything was full of nitrites. Anna heard plenty of lectures at the Senior Citizens' Center, she was an informed woman. Chicken fat could kill you, cream cheese, sour cream, bacon; for years these foods had tempted her to stay alive. When her sister Gert had come with her to the Center for the lecture by the nutritionist, bacon had been the day's main subject. The old man Bernie, who was at the Center all the time, announced that if you drank orange juice when you ate bacon, something in the juice would cancel out the cancer. Gert had poked Anna and muttered, "Jews—all of these Jews—they have no business eating bacon anyway. No business even *talking* about it!"

"Look, get modern, will you?" Anna had said to her. "Get with the twentieth century. You're still living back in the horse-and-buggy age."

"At least people were decent then," Gert had insisted. "Not like this sewer we live in now. Don't invite me to any more lectures. I'm better off at home."

The fumes from the Armenians' patio were filling Anna's apartment, choking her. "Who needs the Gestapo when you have this?" She dragged her kitchen chair into the walk-in pantry closet and closed the door, sitting there in the dark with the matzo meal boxes and the cans of soup. The stink of the charcoal lighter filled every crevice. "What should I do?" she said aloud into the darkness. "Run away three times a day to walk up and down Santa Monica Boulevard till they finish their steaks? Get myself mugged while they eat like horses on my tax money? They should only choke." She hoped the charred meat would work fast on them.

What had *happened* to America, anyway? After seventy-five years of running away from the East Side of New York

. . . . .

with all those barbarians, here she was again with *these*. No progress. All that culture she thought was out there in the world, that she had tried to absorb, came to nothing—to this. What did the world care that Anna Goldman lived in two rooms, and in each room she had a piano!

There was a thud against the wall of the closet. She felt she had been hit in the kidneys.

"Wally, I swear—I'll bite off your little finger if you ever do that again!"

Another thud. The gay young men next door. She knew their pattern. A loud yelling fight, full of accusations. Dishes breaking. Furniture sliding around. Then the 25 lengthy reconciliation, with those noises! Worse than cats in heat. Wasn't it embarrassing for them to meet her at the trash bin after they had carried on like that? Howls, gasps, shrieks, moans! *"Oh my God, oh my God, oh my God,"* one of them always screamed a hundred times. They should only do it in a church where God could hear them, Anna thought, and give me some peace. But when she met one or the other of them at the garbage bin, so well-groomed in his pink silk shirt, or his net underwear, he'd always graciously lift the lid for her, toss her garbage into the back, where she couldn't reach, wish her a good day. At least those boys had manners. They were raised in good American families. But she wouldn't go so far as to let them pull her grocery cart up the steps to her apartment. The last thing she needed was AIDS. She had read in the *LA Times* about the bathhouses in San Francisco, the catwalks where men would stand so others could do a specialized activity on them. Well, that was their business. She was modern, live and let live. Not like Gert, out of the dark ages. But did she have to listen to it all day? She had stopped eating out altogether except for the Center because so many of those gay boys worked in the restaurants. They had a knack for cooking. But did she want them laying lettuce on her tuna sandwiches? Not after where those hands had been!

She opened the closet door; the fumes enclosed her and she could almost feel the flames on her skin, crisping it like bacon.

"Bastards," she whispered. In her old age she should come to this, locked in a closet, instead of revered, respected, with her children gathered round. "They have their own lives to live," she corrected herself. They were loving and loyal, her daughters called her every day. She didn't want to live near them, the way Gert urged her to do—live in the suburbs with a church on every corner and listen to the leaf-blowers blast out her eardrums. The expert on high blood pressure at the Center had lectured on how noise raises the blood pressure of rats within two hours. He should only be here today listening to the racket from the Russian's apartment—he would have a stroke in five minutes.

"Enough of the dark," she said. She stepped out of the closet and heard her doorbell shrilling.

"Who is it?" she yelled, standing ten feet back from the door.

"It's only your landlady, darling, it's not a mugger. Open the door, Mrs. Goldman—we have something to talk about here."

Bitch face Anna thought. *I am not in the mood for this now.* She unlocked her three locks and drew the chain back. "I was just going out, Mrs. Blungman. I give a concert today. Can you make it fast?"

"At our age you shouldn't be in such a hurry," she said, "or it could kill you one-two-three." Mrs. Blungman was short and fat, like a matzo ball. Her face was a lump of dough, with a nose plopped on, two eyes gouged out, and cold blue marbles pressed in the holes. Her hair was thin, like white cotton thread pasted on a child's pink rubber ball.

"I have a complaint against you."

"Who made it?" Anna demanded.

"My sources are confidential. By the way, could it be it was you picked a lemon from my lemon tree?"

"Of course not! Why would I take one of your precious lemons?"

"Lemons are very expensive now in the stores."

"For your information, Mrs. Blungman, I could afford to pay a *dollar* for a lemon if I had to."

"So it wasn't you?"

"So I said."

"So, now to the complaint."

"That wasn't the complaint?"

"The complaint is coming, don't worry, it's right here on my tongue." 27

"Make it fast please. I'm on my way out."

"Alone? You of all people should know how dangerous these streets are. Where's your head after being held up at gunpoint in your store! You take big risks, Mrs. Goldman."

"When I'm in the tomb I won't take risks," Anna said.

"You don't sweep your patio," said Mrs. Blungman.

"I don't sweep my patio? You send spies up to my patio? It's two feet by two feet—I never go out there. No one can see it. The sun never shines there. It stinks from the Armenians' barbecue. I pay rent for my privacy. My patio is my kingdom just like my bathroom."

"So—since you raised the subject yourself, I wasn't going to discuss that today—I would like to know how come there are scratches in your toilet bowl? You clean it with Brillo? We don't allow that."

Anna felt her blood bubble up through her veins.

"You go snooping in my toilet? That's illegal. I could sue you."

"It's legal, darling, for a landlord to have a key to every apartment, in case of fire, to paint, to fix the air conditioner."

"You haven't painted in five years. The air conditioner has been broken since I moved in . . ."

. . . . .

Mrs. Blungman cut her off. "And we could evict you, Mrs. Goldman, if you don't keep your windows open from now on. Because for some crazy reason you keep them all locked up when you go out, and that causes termites in the building."

"*That's ridiculous! That's insane! You're the one who's crazy! Termites if I close my windows!*" Anna began to close the door. Mrs. Blungman stopped her with a heavy hand.

"I didn't get to the main complaint yet, darling."

"Your time is up. I have to go somewhere."

"They don't like your piano playing in the next building."

"Who says so?"

"I got sources. Not every apartment would allow two pianos for one tenant. You have twenty fingers?"

"I told you—one is from the antique store. When I had to give it up, I took the piano from the store here. But I only play one piano at a time. And with the soft pedal, always."

"The people in the next building don't like what you play."

"*What?* You want me to submit a program to them for approval?"

"You play too gloomy. If they have to listen they would like a few show tunes, a patriotic march, something from Barbra Streisand. Not what you give them."

"Mozart you can't give them," Anna said. "Of this I am aware."

"You live on a high horse, Mrs. Goldman. Relax a little, enjoy."

"As long as I sweep my patio and clean my toilet."

"You got it, darling."

Anna walked toward the Senior Citizens' Center. The streets swarmed with foreigners. She could be anywhere— Korea, Israel, Mexico, China. English was no longer the main language of this country. Even on Fairfax Avenue, Yiddish was getting buried. She would go into a bakery, and the women working there were wearing babushkas and jabbering in Russian. She would go to the doctor's office, and the technicians told jokes in Spanish. On top of this, the respectful separation of the sexes was gone—to have a cardiogram she had to submit to a black man snapping his fingers as he plopped rubber suction cups around the edges of her breasts. Her poor misled father, with his dreams of coming to America where the streets were paved with gold. Where anyone could become president (but not a Jew, he realized before he died young). He worked so hard, sewing all day in the factories, bringing home piecework at night. But here the foreigners came with jewelry hidden in their underwear, took their doles from the government, and broiled steaks on their barbecues while Anna choked. The foreigners thought life was a big joke—they were always laughing on the streets. Israeli men wearing gold chains in layers around their hairy necks pushed their dark-eyed, round-nosed babies up and down the streets in fancy strollers. In the city college where Anna took classes, the students with their slanty eyes or their gold-toned skin or their peasant faces all seemed slack, tired, indifferent. Their grades were barely C's. None of them were like the immigrants she was descended from. *They* had worked like demons, learning the language, learning the ways of the new world. These people came and had it handed to them. They came to America poor, but they wouldn't work hard. They wouldn't learn English.

A few years ago when Anna had had her surgery, the Filipino nurses in the hospital had joked in their jabbering tongue, right over her head as if she were nothing more than a tree trunk in the bed, completely ignored her as they wired her into the transfusion machinery; they gossiped nonstop, joked—didn't have the proper respect for their work, for life and death, and for patients who were fighting for one over the other. They thought it was just a big party over here, that's all.

Anna didn't care, as Gert did, about morals, wasn't horrified by the prostitutes strutting up and down Hollywood Boulevard, or by the gay men screaming *oh my God* at their heights of passion. Sex was one thing. She could live with it if she had to, as long as no one was seducing her. But laziness, pure greed and laziness, that was something else.

"Where you been keeping yourself all my life, Sweet Lips?"

30   "I have no patience for you today, Bernie," Anna said, taking her tray, and moving along the lunch line. She only came to the Center because if she ate a real meal at lunchtime (and who could deny that seventy-five cents was a good price?) she wouldn't have to worry about cooking anything for her dinner. She weighed just under a hundred pounds—a fact which was both a source of pride and worry. If she should catch the flu, and not be able to eat for a week, she had no margin to depend on, she would turn into a skeleton. But compared to the matzo-ball ladies all over the place, she had the edge—a certain grace, a swing of her skirt. Bernie wasn't the only one after her. She could see herself in the mirror behind the cafeteria workers—her white hair perfectly short, clipped in a clean, even line. Not a single curl, a pompadour, a frizz; not a bleached mop, not a wig, not a movie-star's head of hair on the face of a crone. Integrity was what she stood for. She was a lost soul, one of a kind, and no one cared about what she stood for.

"White meat of the chicken, please," Anna said.

"Take what's on the plate or leave it, darling," the woman said. "You don't get special privileges."

"Listen, you *know* me," Anna said. "I volunteer my time at this Center just like you, I play a concert here every week. Today in fact."

The woman shoved the plate at her. Diamonds sparkled

on her fingers. "A leg and a wing, darling—that's what's on this plate. Take it or leave it."

Bitch face Anna thought. Give them a little authority and they become like prison wardens. Mrs. Blungmans were everywhere. Sadistic. Vicious. The human race was too far gone. This woman was one of the worst, with her airs and her Zsa-Zsa accent.

Bernie sat next to her. His hands shook as he spread his napkin across his stained gray pants-legs. "My offer is still good, Angel Face," he said, beginning to lift a forkful of peas to his mouth. By the time he got the fork halfway up, most of the peas had spilled off. Anna brushed a pea angrily from her skirt.

"We'll take a cruise to Europe, just you and me, first-class, we'll dance the night away, Emerald Eyes."

She'd been through this before. She'd had a vision of herself in the middle of the ocean, with his corpse on the bed and the band playing "God Bless America" in the grand ballroom. ("A millionaire wants to marry me," Anna had told her daughters. "He has no children—you girls could be rich." "Don't sell your soul for us," the girls had advised her. "Don't worry," Anna had replied. "I wouldn't dream of it.")

The creamed corn was like glue. The chicken leg had a bone showing through, jagged, with black blood clotted in its marrow. Anna reached for her milk carton; her thumbs pressed the edges back and pain shot into both her elbows. She clamped her teeth and waited for it to pass. She didn't need reminders from her nerve endings of what was going on inside her.

"You're doing the wrong end," Bernie said, grease on his chin. "Here, I'll do it for you, Sweet Lips."

She pushed the carton toward him. Bernie couldn't open the milk container either. He was struggling intently, his tongue showing, breathing loudly, pulling at the cardboard with his gnarled fingers. Anna felt her mouth turn down, and tears, like burning acid rising too high from her empty stomach, seared her eyes.

She stood up. Her lunch lay congealing on the paper plate. She touched Bernie on the shoulder, gently.

He didn't turn his head to look up at her; he had arthritis of the neck bones. "I'll be down at the rec room at your concert, Gorgeous," he said. "I'll be there in ten minutes, front row, center. You'll know me by the red rose in my lapel."

In the bathroom Anna combed her hair and saw in the mirror her father's dream—the girl with long sugar-water curls, the girl raised up in the land of opportunity who could play so beautifully the piano he had worked for years to buy her. He wouldn't know her now if he saw her. The skin of her face was an accordion of the days of her life, folded one upon the other. This was what was left of her. What counted was inside, invisible.

Carrying her music, swinging her skirt, she went down the long empty hall to the rec room. The piano keys had only half their ivories. The keyboard welcomed her with its toothless grin.

She knew what they liked, her ten or twelve regulars and the four or five other poor souls who wandered into the rec room, passing time till the free blood pressure test or the cholesterol lecture. They liked "Fiddler on the Roof," "The Entertainer," "Roll Out the Barrel." She knew: *Mozart you can't give them*—but this was her show. It might do them some good. She opened her music book and warmed up her fingers.

THE
BLOOD PRESSURE BUNCH
AND THE
ALZHEIMER'S GANG

At the Multi-Purpose Center there was a bigger crowd for Anna's concert than usual; free blood pressure readings started in an hour—this allowed time for the sediment of the subsidized lunch to settle. The old folks were shuffling their way into the rec room like a herd of cows. Lowing and mooing, scrambling for seats, they were giving their own concert, a regular barnyard symphony—what did they need Anna for?

She ran a few scales up and down the keys of the old spinet; it was badly out of tune, but what did they know—these peasants and barbarians who came to hear her. When the scraping of canes and the whirring of wheel chairs had quieted, she played a few bars of the theme from *Dragnet* to get everyone's attention. Then she swung around on the bench.

"Ladies and gentlemen"—she was as cordial as their round vacant cow-eyes would permit—"today I will be playing a program of Beethoven, Mozart, and Chopin."

A crackling noise in the first row directed Anna's attention to an old man in a wheel chair who was burrowing intently in a brown paper bag in his lap. "Excuse *me*," Anna said. He extracted a bagel which he held up to the light, examining it for defects. "Sir, the lunch hour is over. I ask that no eating take place during the concert."

He appeared not to hear her.

"I just *loathe* Beethoven," said a loud voice from somewhere in the back. This took Anna's breath away. She searched unbelievingly for a face in this room which knew enough to speak the word *loathe.*

"Who said that?" she demanded. "Who?"

"Me." A frizzy blonde, wearing green pants and a pink blouse, stood up. "Beethoven you could die of from boredom. Can't you do a nice tune from *Chorus Line?*"

"I don't know *Chorus Line,*" Anna said. "Sit down please."

The woman stared at her. "You don't know *Chorus Line?* It's only been the biggest hit on Broadway for the last fifty years!"

"I don't specialize in Broadway," Anna said. "Would you please sit down so we can get started?"

"Yeah, sit down!" Bernie yelled. Anna's buddy: he winked at her four times. Or maybe it was the tic from his neuralgia. "Sit down or you get bounced out of here."

Anna waited. She made it clear she would stand there till they behaved. What could she expect in the way of decorum, manners, taste? They were from the jungle. Even when Anna went to the Music Center to hear the greats, the audience applauded at the wrong time—at the end of a movement, sometimes even at a rest in the music. Right in front of her at this very moment, the old man in the wheelchair—could a person believe this?—was smearing his bagel with cream cheese from a little paper cup balanced on his knee.

"You," Anna said. "The gentleman right here. *You! There is no eating allowed in this room.*"

"Oh—give him a break," the blonde in the pink blouse yelled. "He came too late for lunch, they wouldn't let him in. So let him have his little snack."

The man was chewing quite happily. He smiled at Anna, gratefully, sweetly, his eyes bright. Like a little monkey, he looked at her from under his bushy eyebrows. All right, he was from the Alzheimer's Gang, he didn't know any better.

34

. . . . .

Anna swung back around on her seat and brushed her hands delicately over her skirt. She positioned her hands and began to play the first notes of the "Moonlight Sonata." Immediately a scuffling started up behind her; she threw a fast look over her shoulder.

"What is this?" she cried, stopping at once.

"Play, honey, play," said a woman of no less than ninety years. She was spinning around on the floor. "You make my heart happy. When do I ever get a chance to dance like this?" She waltzed in a circle by herself, holding a bulging shopping bag against her chest.

Anna looked around to see if there was someone, anyone, who could understand her exasperation with a lunatic like this. But all of them had the same blank innocent eyes— cows chewing their cud. There was no way to get respectful attention here. No way at all.

"Please, please!" Anna said. "Sit down. If you want to dance, join the dance class."

"I'm all done, darling," the old woman said. "My breath is gone. My pacemaker only lets me celebrate a few seconds at a time. So don't worry, I'm all done. Relax. Sit down now and play some more, send us to seventh heaven."

Anna Goldman and Arthur Rubinstein were the only two people in the world who knew what a battle it was to get the attention of the mindless masses.

"The piano has a little look of a coffin," Rubinstein said a few years ago on the *MacNeil-Lehrer Report*. At home Anna had a typed copy (she sent away two dollars to the television station) of what Rubinstein had said in the interview. She kept it on her coffee table and read it every day for support. Arthur would certainly sympathize with her right now if he were here. He knew how hard it was, he said it himself: how people came to listen to him play after a good dinner, the women thinking only about dresses, the men about business or sports. *"There I have this crowd, not really knowers of music . . . and that is a very difficult*

proposition. I have to hold them . . . by my emotion . . .
there is a moment where I please them all . . . I can hold
them with one little note in the air, and they will not
breathe. . . . That is a great, great moment. Not always
does it happen, but when it does happen, it is a great
moment of our lives."

Well, it didn't ever happen at the Multi-Purpose Center.
Anna wished Arthur Rubinstein were her husband. She
would leave here and go home, and there he'd be on her
little worn-out couch, waiting for her, sipping tea, listening
to music in his head. She would tell him about the crazies at
her concert, and he'd commiserate, nod his head, say,
"Well, you're doing them good, music is good for their
souls." He would think they had souls. She didn't.

She really *could* have married him. He was born in 1887,
only twenty years before she was. She could have met him,
they would have had brilliant children, great musicians.
Not that she hadn't loved her Abram, not that she didn't
love her girls, but her musical gene had been diluted to
nothing in her children by Abram, a sweet man but not an
artist, a man who couldn't play a note. The girls didn't turn
out to have one drop of musical talent. When they were
little she would threaten them: "I'm going to swallow iodine
if you don't sit down and practice." She and Arthur
Rubinstein had the same passionate nature—they were
both from Polish stock. Like Anna with her iodine, he had
tried to kill himself when he was twenty because he had no
money and he was in love with a married woman who
wouldn't get a divorce. Hanging himself didn't work—the
things he used broke—so he sat down and played the piano
instead. Anna understood this exactly; that's what she always did. When it became clear to her (which it did every
day) that life was all a big nothing, she sat down and played
the piano. So here she was: playing for the Blood Pressure
Bunch and the Alzheimer's Gang.

She surrendered herself to the notes of the "Moonlight
Sonata" and pretended Rubinstein was watching her from

the poster on the wall that said "High Blood Pressure Is the Silent Killer"—he was listening to her, his beautiful long head cocked slightly to the side. She closed her eyes, feeling the pedals rise and fall under her feet. She had a sense of herself as a ballerina, lightly moving over a green meadow. Rubinstein was admiring the way her delicate shoulders swayed, the way her girlish waist bent, the airy movement of the hem of her skirt. Her face, her ancient, fallen face, was bowed over the keys, hidden from view. Even her hands, whose skin was as crinkled and brown as the bag which held the old man's bagel, moved like graceful white birds. All that she was was in the music.

"Bravo, Passion Flower!"

Oh, shut up, Bernie!

"Come to my tent tonight!" he called.

Men and their circulating hormones. They never gave up. Even Rubinstein was probably dreaming of it when he was ninety-five. Abram had looked forward to it, every night if she would let him, not really believing that the next day she always had a migraine. Even when she had a migraine, and told him so, he'd say, "I'll make it better. I'll kiss it away." Beethoven probably had it on his mind all the time, too. Otherwise, how could he write music like this? The calm after the struggle, the peace in the moonlight.

When it was over, when she had grudgingly played "Sunrise, Sunset" as her encore, she began to gather up her music.

"That was very good, I want you to know you have talent," the blonde in the green pants said to Anna. "Would you be interested in a blind date? You look like you could use a little social life."

"I look somehow lacking to you?" Anna asked. The woman had wrists and ankles like an ox, a peasant face.

"You look good for your age, you kept your weight down," the woman said.

"Thank you."

. . . . .

"The man I have in mind for you is my neighbor. He's in the hospital now with his prostate. But a wonderful musician. When he gets out is what I'm thinking—he used to play the tuba in the Cleveland Symphony before his emphysema."

"He'll need a nurse when he gets out," Anna said.

"So—what's the harm if you make a little chicken soup till he's on his feet? This is a wonderful man I'm talking about, a prize."

"If he's so wonderful, why don't you have a social life with him?"

38   "I'm dating a butcher, thank you," she said. "Kosher. The finest cuts of meat."

"Meat at our age is very bad," Anna said. "Don't you listen at the lectures? And will you please excuse me now?" Anna said. "I'm very tired."

"He would appreciate your thin hips. His wife, she should rest in peace, was a hippopotamus down there."

"Excuse me," Anna said. "I'm not feeling well."

"It's the food they serve us here. Surplus from World War Two, I think."

Bernie was now closing in on her; she had the impression that he was flapping his lips like a goldfish.

"Look!" Anna pointed to the door. "They're lining up for blood pressure! You two don't want to miss it. High blood pressure is the silent killer."

Anna sat at her kitchen table and ate a chocolate chip cookie. No Arthur Rubinstein was on her couch. It was getting dark and the gay boys next door were playing "The Tennessee Waltz." Her daughters were probably cooking dinner in their houses, something warm and nourishing, possibly even stuffed cabbage, which it seemed to her she had last made in another life. Her girls—an hour away in the suburbs—always said, "We wish you lived nearby, then you could have dinner with us." They didn't know what

they were saying. If she lived nearby, there would be no end
of complications. For example, Janet's husband, the professor, had a habit of chewing his applesauce. This annoyed
Anna and she would probably have to say something eventually. Her other son-in-law had had much worse habits—
and to him she had said plenty—but he was dead. She
sometimes thought she should move in with Carol and help
her raise the boys.

Neither of the boys could spell the simplest words; they
had never even *heard* of Beethoven—all they cared about
was some ugly gorilla called Hulk Hogan. Also, they de-
voured food like King Kong. They lived—like some new **39**
mutation of penguins—in the refrigerator. Whenever Anna
looked at them, two healthy boys, they always had an arm
stuck in the freezer, pulling out frozen pizzas, frozen burritos, frozen donuts, and always—the other hand wrapped
around a can of soda, as if milk didn't exist. They had
things in and out of the microwave so fast, it was like
watching a speeded-up film. Anna was appalled to see that
much food disappear down their gullets. No one needed to
eat that much, that constantly. She was sure most of it
passed out of their systems undigested. And their mother
let them get away with it. It was true Carol had other things
on her mind; she had to devote a great deal of time going to
singles' events and then getting depressed from the losers
she met, but still . . .

There was no point trying to run her children's lives.
From a distance, it was all right to see their flaws and get
annoyed; if she lived with them, she would probably have a
stroke every day from their stupidity. Maybe what she
needed to take her mind off her troubles was a social life.
But did she want a blind date with an invalid tuba player
who had been married to a hippopotamus?

If only Rubinstein were eligible! If only money grew on
trees and everyone were a genius! If Anna decided to go
looking among the hordes, she would have to be very

choosy. She'd seen an interesting ad in the personal column in the paper for the last three weeks. She had it right here on the table:

"Scrabble Expert welcomes challenge from Smart Cookie. Former Navy officer with medals, now senior citizen; owns seventeen dictionaries. Non-smoking gentleman. Wordsmith. Elocution afficionado. Will come to you. Or vice-versa. Call 653-1050."

At least here was a man who knew a word or two. These days, even that was a miracle.

40   "I'm rapturous that you called, you sound very intelligent," the man said on the phone. "You want to elucidate and maybe give your name?"

"Not yet. I don't reveal my name to strangers so fast," Anna said.

"You want your nomenclature to be 'Hey you'?"

"Slow down," Anna said. "You live alone?"

"A widower for ten years, tired of solitary hibernation. I have impressive references if you want; I'm clean living, no drinking, no gambling. My late wife was an angel; I respect women, believe me, so I'm not looking for funny-business."

"What are you looking for?"

"Companionship, a good game of Scrabble, maybe a steak dinner out now and then."

"Steak is a death sentence at our age," Anna said. "You're how old?"

"A young seventy-three. And you?"

"Around there," Anna said. "In very good shape."

"You have a pencil? I'll give you directions."

"How could you imagine I would come to a perfect stranger's house? How do I know you have honorable intentions?" On the last words Anna's voice had turned coy and flirtatious, which astonished her—that such a tone still lived within her.

"That's very perspicacious of you. I respect caution these

days. So let me get a pencil—you'll give me directions to your place."

"What about your seventeen dictionaries—you carry them with you?"

"On the bus that would be foolish."

"I'm thinking suddenly this is a mistake," Anna said. "Nice as I'm sure you are, I can't let a perfect stranger come to my house."

"If I'm perfect, what's the worry?"

Anna was silent. She considered hanging up.

"I'm sorry," he said. "A bad choice of a joke."

"I'll think about this and call you in a few days."

"No! Don't hang up! Please! Let's not lose this propitious event."

"You don't have many calls on your ad?"

"Not from a cultured, charming person with expertise like yourself, who sounds like twenty years old."

"All right," Anna said. "I have an idea. We could meet at the Multi-Purpose, you know the one on Fairfax?"

"Certainly I do. Tomorrow?"

"I could arrange it. After lunch. In the lobby. One o'clock."

"I'll bring Scrabble."

"Good," Anna said.

"So now, would you consider it wise to tell me your name?"

"Anna Goldman."

"How do you do, Anna?"

"And you go by . . .?"

"Jack . . . Jack or Izzy Fine, take your pick, what suits your inclinations."

"Thank you," Anna said. "Jack is fine."

"I'll count the minutes, already my stopwatch is running," he said.

Anna laughed in spite of herself. Then she carefully lowered her voice and said goodbye sternly. Still, the instant she hung up, she laughed out loud again. For the briefest moment, everything in her kitchen looked bright, as if little lights had gone on inside her teapot, her sugar bowl, and her toaster oven.

But when she actually saw him in the lobby, spiffy in a sport jacket, his two strands of white hair glued to his spotted brown scalp, her throat closed. She knew him by the Scrabble set in his lap. But aside from that, she knew him. By his high waist, by his thin legs, by his flabby arm muscles. She knew him the same way she knew the legions of old ladies—she knew his story: the dead wife, the kids (he'd have complaints about them or he'd rave about how good they were to him). Either he was lonely, or he had ten old ladies making propositions of marriage every day. Or not *even* of marriage—of anything! There were eighty-five women for every fifteen decrepit, on-their-last-legs old men in this town, and most of them were shameless!

Anna wobbled forward on her high heels toward the row of orange chairs, one of which contained Jack Fine. She could break an ankle from this vanity. The smell of the perfume she had sprayed on her neck was choking her. Her skirt had little gold threads woven through it which caught the ceiling lights and flashed reflections up at her to give her the symptoms she'd been warned about by Dr. Rifkin: the way it would feel when her retina detached. Her blind date was sitting rigid, clutching a battered brown Scrabble box. His tie, bright red, dotted with white anchors, was knotted so high under his chin it appeared to be cutting off his air. His face was mottled with matching red circles—probably a symptom of impending stroke. She could tell he was wearing a laundry-starched shirt to impress her. A gold tie clasp gleamed. She had a vision of him taking off his shirt; in fact, he was suddenly taking off all his clothes right in front of her. They were perhaps already married—or, if she had lowered her standards, maybe going on a cruise together.

But there she was, stuck with him. His spine was sunken between the white slack muscles of his curved back. And the rest—God help her! She didn't want to *imagine* the rest of what she'd see if he took off his pants!

And in between now and the fabulous cruise—the eternity of dinners with him, his false feeth digging into steak after steak! The earliest confiding conversations: which operations he had had, which she had had, which ones he needed, which ones she needed. And the ailments yet to come for both of them! They would never run out of material.

But finally, and most terrifying, as they progressed into **43** their future together, he would have to get it over with. "Play the piano for me, Anna," he would ask, because, if he was any kind of gentleman, if he was decent, he'd have to recognize "her interests." He would lean back on her couch, chivalrous, gallantly stifling his yawns while she was coerced into betraying Mozart for him!

Not a moment too soon she stopped to scrutinize a cholesterol poster: a dead cow and a happy fish. Her beloved Arthur Rubinstein had said that people who think happiness is to enjoy a good cutlet and go to bed and win at a game are stupid. *"There is nothing in it,"* he had said. *"That is not life. Life is bite into it, to take absolutely as it is."*

Jack Fine, a sailor's sappy grin hanging crooked on his face, was sweeping the field with his lighthouse eyes. His beam hit her square in the face and knocked her off course. One second more and Anna might not have escaped. Now it was merely a matter of deserting him at dockside. All right—it wasn't the most refined thing to do, but it wouldn't be such a horror. He'd sit there alone for maybe ten more minutes. By then a half-dozen dames would be closing in, complimenting the anchors on his tie.

COMES AN
EARTHQUAKE

Anna—who never once played a card game in her adult life—leaned back in one of the red metal chairs furnished for the guests of the Colby Plaza and watched her sister Ava hunched over her cards. Anna had been in Miami Beach five days already and was still at a loss to understand Ava and her friends. Furred in mink stoles and intent on their hands, they expertly slid new cards into their fans, closing and opening them like magic. What Anna couldn't understand was how these old ladies—women who'd lived through the Depression, who'd lost sons in the war (Ava's son went down over New Guinea and her youngest boy was peppered with shrapnel in France), women who'd lost a husband or two—could just sit on their behinds eight hours a day on a porch in Miami Beach and play poker!

"I'm wondering . . ." Anna said, "how is it that no one around here ever walks to the beach, only a block away? Where I live, in Los Angeles, you could give your right arm for a breath of air like this."

"So why not move here?" asked one of the ladies. No one raised her head from over her cards; Anna wasn't sure if the voice belonged to Ida (whose husband, Herman, was upstairs with Alzheimer's) or Sadie (emphysema—she smoked four packs a day) or Ava's best friend, Mickey (her husband had had a fatal heart attack when he tripped on two gay boys, naked on the beach at night, a year ago).

"Why should anyone move to a morgue?"

. . . . .

A man's voice. At first Anna thought it came from Collins
Avenue, from the sidewalk five feet in front of her chair
where a trickle of old folks passed by in the deepening
dusk. The women, dragged down by their diamonds and
mink, promenaded, as if along a hospital corridor, on the
arms of old men wearing jackets and bow ties. Anna
glanced along the row of metal chairs till she made out what
looked like a dark balloon floating against the pink stucco
of the hotel wall. She tried to focus her eyes. Glaucoma was
working its way through her retina; one of these days the
sights of the world would go black on her. (Amazing, how
46 this morning, Ava, needing to sew a button on her house-
coat, threaded the needle in just one pass; eyes like an eagle
and she was ninety to Anna's seventy-eight.)

"Irving bubbie, light of my life, go back upstairs or go
across to the Crown and see the show but do us a favor and
shut up," said Sadie.

"Aah, they die like flies here," Irving said. "What's the
point? Tell me," he leaned forward and addressed Anna.
"What is the point of it all?"

Anna squinted, trying to see him better. She made out a
pair of white suede loafers with red rubber soles, some
skinny knees.

"There *is* no point," Anna said in his direction. "You're
right—it's all a big nothing."

"Look around you," he said. "We all come to the last stop
like lemmings running to the ocean. We run to Miami Beach
and play cards with our last breaths. We're dying and
playing cards at the edge of the cliff till we get shoved off."

"You're a sick man?" Anna asked.

"I have AIDS," he said.

"AIDS?" Anna said, shocked. She shut her mouth tightly.
He didn't look like the type, but you could never tell. A
snort came from Ava at the card table.

"Tell her, Irving, what kind of AIDS you have."

"You want to know?" He addressed Anna.

"Don't feel you have to talk about it," she said, trying to breathe very shallowly.

"I'm happy to tell you. I'm able to talk very freely about this." He paused. "I got hearing aids!"

It took a moment for Anna to digest this information. Then she felt taken. She wished fervently she were home in her dark apartment in Los Angeles where the Armenians next door choked her with their barbecue fumes. She had come on this trip to Florida to see Ava one last time before one of them died. Sisters were sisters, after all, and how much time was there? Ava already had a pacemaker and an artificial heart valve. Anna, thank God, had only the usual: arthritis, glaucoma, osteoporosis, high blood pressure, nothing serious.

Irving said, "If you don't laugh, you'll cry, take your pick."

"Serious things like AIDS you shouldn't joke about," Anna insisted. "Have some respect."

"For what? I should take the world seriously? Why should I? What's the world ever given me that's any good except maybe my children?"

"And then even they don't visit," Anna remarked strictly for his benefit only, since her daughters, when she was home in LA, called her every day.

"Not *my* children. My daughter is married to a millionaire," Irving corrected Anna. "She sends a limousine for me every Sunday, I go to eat Chinese, Italian, whatever I want, cost is no object."

Ava called over from the card table, "Tell the truth, Irving. Tell my sister you eat with the chauffeur, not with your daughter. When does *she* come? The last time was when you fell out of the elevator and broke your elbow."

"Never mind. The chauffeur is like a son to me," Irving called back. "Better than a son. Don't lose your concentration, Ava—those cardsharps over there will cheat you blind if they get one chance."

"I'm ahead four dollars, already, Irving," Ava informed him, ". . . and the night is young." Each time, she pronounced his name "Oiving," and Anna winced. The Bronx still lived in full color in Ava—nothing could winnow it out. The Bronx sat on Ava's tongue like a wart. Anna herself was certain she had no trace of any crude accent. She tried to speak like an American descended from someone who came over on the Mayflower.

"Listen to this one," Irving said. "Two old men are playing golf, but their eyes are so bad they can't see where the ball lands. A third *alta cocka* comes by and says he has perfect eyesight, he'll help them out. He'll watch the ball for them. So one of them hits the ball and then asks, 'So did you see where it landed?' The *alta cocka* says, 'Of course I saw, I got perfect eyesight.' 'So where is it?' the golfer says. 'I forgot,' says the old man."

"An Alzheimer joke! For shame!" Sadie said. "With Ida sitting right here and poor Herman upstairs, putting on his socks backwards this minute."

Irving's attention was drawn away as a fire truck and an ambulance raced by, their sirens screaming. "What's your hurry?" Irving asked, waving his hand at them in dismissal.

Anna's eyes had adjusted to the darkness, and she watched Irving's bald head wobbling on his turkey neck. His ears were huge; they hung on his skull like some strange invention. Certain animals, when she saw them on nature programs, made her feel this way. They adapted to their environment without regard for polite shapes. She didn't want to have to look at their hanging pouches or spiky chins or poison sacs. Old people, too, grew strange parts, took on camouflaging skin pigments, adopted peculiar postures and gaits. Anna hated belonging to an indelicate species.

"Another cowboy bites the dust," Irving said as the taillights of the ambulance disappeared. "Who knows who'll be next?"

"Comes an earthquake we'll all be gone," Anna pronounced.

. . . . .

"Here we have hurricanes," Irving told her. "At least get your catastrophes straight."

"A flush!" Ava said with a cry of glee, laying down her cards. She swept the pile of coins in the kitty toward her.

"Believe me, you can't take it with you," Irving predicted. "Slow down, Ava, enjoy the sights."

"I'm done, anyway . . . it's time for us to go up," Ava said. "*Wheel of Fortune* is on in five minutes." The four ladies pushed back their chairs and stood up. Ava tapped the cards into a neat little square and set the deck down on the table. She gathered up her big pile of quarters and dropped them in the jacket of her flowered pantsuit. She adjusted her mink.

"You ladies live by the game shows," Irving said. "But look, right here, isn't life the biggest game show of all?"

"You're giving away trips to Hawaii?" Sadie asked him. "If you're giving away free cruises, we'll stay and watch you."

"I told you before, Sadie—you want a cruise, I'll take you on a cruise."

"When I'm that desperate, I'll let you know."

"I'm going upstairs now, Anna," Ava said. "Come with me."

"Maybe I'll stay here a while. I could do without the *Wheel of Fortune*," Anna said.

Ava shot her a look, the same kind of look she'd sent her when Anna had been flower girl at Ava's wedding in 1914 and stepped on her train, causing Ava to stumble. "Come up," Ava demanded. "Irving sits here all night. Irving is always here. You'll see him when we come down again from nine to ten to watch the sideshow going by," Ava assured her.

"Your sister thinks this is the army, she lives by a schedule," Irving mumbled into the dark. Anna had noticed this was true: Ava woke at eight, ate toast dipped in coffee poured into her saucer, watched the *$25,000 Pyramid*, watched *Cardsharks*, watched the daytime *Wheel of For-*

tune, came down for poker till Meals on Wheels arrived, ate lunch from Styrofoam boxes with the other ladies on the porch (a drumstick, yellow wax beans, a slice of white bread, a cup of bouillon soup and some Jell-O). After lunch, a nap, then an *I Love Lucy* rerun, then down to the porch for card playing till dinnertime, then up for dinner, then down again for cards, then up again for TV, then down again for one last blast of bus fumes on the porch. On certain days there were doctor appointments, and once a week the trip in Hyman Cohen's hotel station wagon to the Food Circus.

50   As Anna walked by Irving's big feet to follow Ava into the lobby, he reached out for her hand. He had the nerve to grab it and squeeze it for a couple of seconds before he let it go. She looked down into his blue eyes and saw him smiling up at her. "Laugh a little, sweetheart," he said. "There's no good jokes six feet under."

A strange sensation woke Anna; the room glowed blue with particles of light reflected from the shimmering signs of the Crown and the Cadillac. No air came in the lowered windows. Ava never ran the air conditioner: she said it was too noisy, but Anna knew it was the expense. Ava had always been a miser. When they had talked long distance, arranging the visit, Ava had promised Anna a room of her own "right across the hall from mine, one with its own TV," but when Anna had arrived at the Colby Plaza, the first thing Ava said was, "I got a cot in my room for you so you wouldn't have to be all alone. It worried me, you should be all alone in a strange place."

The cot is cheaper, Anna thought, but then was sorry to think badly of her sister who was soon, no doubt, to depart this vale of tears. Ava lay only a foot away breathing noisily through her open mouth. The segments of her false teeth shone like some plastic toy. The room made Anna feel claustrophobic: two beds, a stove, a sink, a refrigerator, a dining table, a dresser, a TV, a recliner chair. All Ava's worldly goods were here; from her huge, human life—a husband, children, big decisions to make—to this: *Wheel of Fortune*, Meals on Wheels, poker, little tiny portions of milk frozen in margarine containers to last the week. (Anna already lived this way in LA; it wasn't news to her but to see that her powerful sister had come to this was a shock.)

She tried to go back to sleep. She kept remembering how Irving had grabbed her hand. An old turkey. A no one. Still, his fingers had felt alive. There was heat and strength in them. She had felt something, a feeling. This was astonishing, to feel something and to think about it. To bother to think about something and to feel pleasure from it.

Anna tiptoed out of bed, put on her clothes, and went down in the old elevator to the lobby. The light of dawn was just arriving through the windows; the desk clerk, a Cuban named Jesús who always wore a dirty black suit, was sleeping on one of the old couches. Anna didn't know what to do with herself. The cards from last night, she saw, were still on the table outside. She could play solitaire. She could actually walk to the ocean and watch the sunrise.

Would it be dangerous? To go alone to the beach? Did they have muggers in Miami Beach? Never mind muggers, she would go anyway. At her age forget everything. Doom was just as likely hiding in her arteries as on the sand.

Irving was still outside on the front porch, sleeping in his chair, his head back against the stucco wall. Had he really been there all night? Anna stared. She thought she could see dew condensed on his bald head. His white shoes glowed in the dimness. Maybe he was dead. She went over to him and tapped on his skull. He jerked upright.

"Dummy," she said with relief. "You don't have a bed?"

"I wasn't sleeping," he said, straightening his eye glasses. "Just taking the air."

"Who cares?" Anna said. "I'm going beachcombing."

"I'll come with you."

51

. . . . .

"I'm going alone," Anna said. "I need an adventure. When did I ever see the sunrise? In California, you only get sunsets. And at the end of the day, who's going to run to the beach?"

"Here no one runs, we all walk," Irving explained, as he creaked himself out of the chair. He offered Anna his arm. "But allow me to come along and be your bodyguard."

They saw it happen, a fuzz of pink over the blue horizon, a blur of white cloud, and then the emerging burning ball, coming up on a fountain of flame.

52   "That alone," Irving said, standing against the rail of the narrow boardwalk while seagulls screeched and wheeled overhead, ". . . and you could believe in God."

"You believe?" Anna asked.

"What am I, some kind of sucker?"

"Smart people, really smart people—some of them are believers."

"I'll take my medicine straight," Irving said. "I'll face the firing squad without a blindfold."

"It would be nice to believe something," Anna said. "Then you could have reasons, you could have meaning, you could have a social center, you could have someone to say a prayer when you're dead. This way, like for my husband Abram, I had to hire a stranger, a baby calling himself a rabbi, he reads from a printed sheet 'This was a good man, a good husband, a good father.' A know-nothing."

"If I were going to believe, I'd choose Jesus," Irving said. "He's the best deal around. But no one in Miami Beach, Florida, in the Jew-nited States of America, thinks he's worth two cents."

"They prefer Moses?"

"He can't hold a candle. All he did was talk to God in the burning bush. The trouble is, when you're this old, you should have something to hang on to."

. . . . .

"How old?"

"Ninety-two," Irving said. "Come June."

"My husband died at fifty-five," Anna said. "You had a whole lifetime extra over him."

"It's never enough," Irving said. "It doesn't feel like I even started yet."

They began to walk along the wooden boardwalk. Two seagulls lit on the railing and walked right up to them. They stared boldly, craning their beaks forward.

"They want something," Anna said.

"So who doesn't?" Irving answered. The sun was well out of the ocean now, getting redder.

"Look," Anna said. "Is that beautiful or is that beautiful?"

"You're what's beautiful," Irving said.

"Don't get carried away, Irving," Anna said. "My week is up. I'm going home tomorrow, and anyway I'm not available."

"My mistake. The first day I saw you on the porch we should have got acquainted. I should have talked to you sooner. You got a boyfriend?"

"My heart belongs to Arthur Rubinstein," Anna said.

"He's younger than me? Richer?"

"Never mind," Anna said. "It's not going anywhere with Arthur and me."

"Even at our age we have a right to pleasure," Irving said.

"Don't lump yourself together with me," Anna said. "You're old enough to be my father. Look how you can hardly walk and I'm limber on my toes like a ballet dancer."

"It's these rubber soles," he explained. "New shoes. They glue me down. It's like wearing suction cups."

"You want to go on the sand?" Anna asked. "You want to stick your toes in the water?"

"In my heart, I'm running down to the waves already,"

. . . . .

Irving said, stopping to lean on the rail, breathing hard. "I'm splashing you with water. I'm ducking you under."

"And I'm jumping over waves," Anna said, looking out at the blue wide ocean.

"I'm tickling you," Irving said.

"I'm laughing," Anna said. She turned her head away from him.

"So how come you're crying?" Irving asked after a minute.

"Because it's a pity," Anna said, wiping her eyes with a tissue. "What we used to have, and what we can't have anymore."

"At least let's take what we can get," Irving said. He held out his hand. Anna studied it. Then she crooked her fingers in his. He brought their hands up to his mouth and kissed Anna's fingers. "I'm doing more than this with you," he said. "Much more. You understand what I mean?"

"Don't have a dirty mind," Anna said.

"I'm doing everything," Irving said. "Every sweet thing. We're in heaven."

Anna was silent.

"I'm going too far?" Irving asked.

"No," Anna said. "I appreciate it."

The next afternoon, the last of her visit, when the Red Top Cab had been called and was to pick her up in one hour for the trip to the airport, Anna put on her new silky flowered dress and got everything else into her suitcase. Ava was already down on the front porch playing cards. Anna realized that if she stayed here for a year, the sister business wouldn't improve. Ava wasn't going to get sentimental. A big bossy sister stays a big bossy sister. To cheer herself up, she sprayed herself five times with Ava's expensive perfume, and by the time she rode down in the elevator with her suitcase she smelled like a lilac tree. She would be lucky if in two minutes there weren't bees landing all over her head.

. . . . .

Irving was spiffy in a plaid jacket and a red bow tie.

He saluted her from his chair. "Forgive me if even on this farewell occasion I don't stand up," he said. "One knee isn't so good today."

"Stand up anyway, Irving," Ava called over to him. "Use it or you'll lose it."

"He lost it already," Sadie said, with a hoarse laugh. "Otherwise I'd go with him on a cruise."

"I didn't lose it, sweetheart," he said, getting red in the face. "I just don't give it away to big-mouth yentas." He turned to Anna. "You're lucky you're getting out of here. If I could go with you, I'd run in a minute."

"So where am I going that's so special?" Anna said, suddenly seeing a picture in her mind of her tiny dark apartment, of her pianos, two of them, with the lids down over the keys, of the milk going sour in the refrigerator.

"Maybe you could get a room here," Irving suggested. "You know," he called over to the ladies at the card table, "I don't think Hyman rented the room yet from after when Sam Kriskin died."

"No thank you," Anna said. "I'm not interested in living in a dead man's room."

"He didn't die in the room," Irving assured her. "Only on the way in the ambulance. Not a single bad thing happened in the room. Kriskin was an immaculate person. That man was as clean as holy water."

"What's the rent?" Anna said. It was a question she didn't expect to ask. It was meaningless, it was to make talk. It was stupid to have brought it up, what did she care? In LA she had a very good rent-controlled apartment, and, besides, she would never leave her daughters, what for? To come here and sit with some old man?

But Irving's blue eyes shone like electrified marbles, and he was already getting up slowly from the red metal chair. "We'll go in the lobby, Anna," he said. "We'll find out the rent, maybe you'll stay, then what a time we'll have, you and I—we'll go across to the Crown every night and watch the floor show, we'll go out to dinner on Sundays with my daughter's chauffeur, we'll buy a VCR and rent a movie . . ."

Irving started to walk without his feet. Anna saw his upper body move toward her, but his shoes, his white shoes with the red rubber soles, stayed glued to the cement and she saw him go down like a boulder.

When she opened her eyes the next instant, he was face down on the cement porch and no one even noticed it. Ava was dealing a new hand of cards.

56   Irving, rolling on his round belly, was silent. He turned his head slightly to the side, and Anna saw his cracked eye glasses and blood on his forehead.

"Oh God," she cried out. "Look over here!"

Irving whimpered a little and stayed on his face.

"Oh—help me pick him up, *please!*" Anna cried. She could not bend down alone because of her osteoporosis and her arthritis and her collapsed vertebrae.

"We don't pick anyone up here," Sadie said from the table. "We each got our own problems. In no time flat we could all land in the hospital."

"They fall here every day," Ida added.

"How many times has Irving fallen anyway?" Mickey asked, and all the women looked skyward, as if they were figuring.

Anna couldn't bear it, to see him gasping and jerking like a beached fish down there, his forehead on cement. She rushed into the lobby and grabbed a cushion from one of the sagging couches. She carried it outside and slid it under Irving's forehead.

"Don't move him," Ava said. "Something could be broken."

"The last time nothing was broken," Ida said.

"But the time before, remember, it was his elbow."

"This was a softer fall than that one. That time, he

stepped out the elevator before it was level. Everyone heard him go down."

Anna ran inside again and yelled to the Cuban clerk. "Jesús! Call the doctor, dummy!" He seemed to be counting out colored postcards of the Colby Plaza. He was counting in Spanish.

Outside again, Anna knelt over Irving. "Irving, can you hear me?" He rocked on his round stomach to answer her. "Are you okay, Irving?" she asked him. "Are you comfortable?"

"I make a nice living," he said.

Anna looked at him, then stood up, shocked.

"A joke," he said. Then he spit out a little blood.

"Jesús!" she yelled into the lobby "Did you call?" The man looked up from the desk, puzzled. It occurred to Anna that he was drunk.

"Hey," he said suddenly. "That old guy can't be on that pillow." He ran out to the porch and grabbed the cushion from under Irving's forehead. "If he bleeds on this, Hyman Cohen will blow a fit! These are his new pillows!"

"Ten years new," Ava called over to them.

"Jesús! Come here!" She called him like a dog, slapping her leg. "Help me pick him up this minute!"

"There's no hurry," the Cuban said. "They'll pick him up when they come."

"Who?"

"The paramedics."

"Did you call them?"

"They have a standing appointment here," Sadie said from the card table as she lit another cigarette.

"Go," Anna said, shoving the Cuban. "Call them!" She watched him till he went in and picked up the phone.

While they waited, Anna sat down on the steps of the Colby Plaza and maneuvered Irving's face, still pointing down, into her lap. She stroked the few hairs on the back of his bald head.

57

. . . . .

"Don't worry, Irving darling," she whispered. "You'll be
fine, this is just a little nothing. We all have days like this. I
myself fell in a hole in a parking lot a year ago. I still have a
bone spur on my foot from it."

Irving was crying.

"It hurts you somewhere? It hurts a lot?"

He nodded his head. His weight in her lap felt like the
weight of one of her babies. She thought the feeling of
taking care had disappeared forever, and now here it was
again.

"Here they come," Ava announced.

58   A shuddering vibration shook the street, and a fire truck
pulled up at the curb. Four firemen jumped off; they were
wearing black rubber trousers with yellow suspenders.

"Aah, it's you again, isn't it?" one of them said to Irving.
Irving was sobbing without restraint now. She could feel his
hot tears seep through her dress. She found his hand and
squeezed it. He held on very tight.

"Don't worry, Irving dear," she whispered into his ear.
"It's only this life-and-death business we're having here.
Don't take it seriously."

The firemen were turning him over, opening a big black
box, taking out rubber tubes, gauze, fancy machines. If the
firemen were being the doctors, then were the doctors running up and down ladders putting out fires?

The paramedics clumped around in their huge rubber
boots. "Anything hurt?" they kept asking Irving. "Where
does it hurt?"

"He's fine," Ava called from the card table. "The man is
made of steel. I warned him, never wear shoes with rubber
soles. And I told him, always get up slow, get your balance
first. But no, a big shot, he was in a hurry to impress my
sister."

Anna shot her a look, like the look Ava had shot Anna in
1914.

"Here comes the ambulance," one of the firemen said.

. . . . .

"Are you going to the hospital with him?" He was addressing Anna.

"Yes," Anna said, and at the same instant Ava called out,
"No, of course she isn't going. Let his daughter go."

"My daughter never comes," Irving cried, crushing
Anna's hand now that he was sitting up, propped by the
firemen.

"I'll come with you," Anna said. "Don't worry,"

"Don't be a fool," Ava said. She was finally talking directly to Anna, paying her the attention that she hadn't
given in the whole visit, pulling her up by the arm. "You'll
have to wait there seven hours. That's how long they make
you wait in Emergency. It's stacked to the ceiling with old
people who fell down."

"I have time," Anna said.

"No you don't," Ava said. "The cab is here,"

Anna had forgotten entirely. The Red Top. The airport.
The plane. LA. Her pianos with the shrouded keys.

"Take her suitcase," Ava instructed the driver who had
come up onto the porch and was staring, open-mouthed, at
Irving. Ava pushed Anna toward the steps. Her mink's
head, slithering on her shoulder, showed its tiny razor-
sharp teeth.

"Take her to the airport," Ava instructed the cab driver.
"And you . . .," she said to the ambulance driver, "you get
going and take *him* to the hospital."

Irving reached out to Anna, and Anna reached for Irving. But the forces were too strong, the time was too late.
They were too powerless. Two minutes later they were rushing in opposite directions—she could feel the wind tearing
them apart, the seagulls were going every which way over
the ocean—and Anna couldn't tell if the sirens she heard
were approaching or receding.

STARRY NIGHT

Looking out the window of the bus, Anna could see a pandemonium of gold and glitter—the whole world rushing around crazily, buying presents. On Wilshire Boulevard, people were stabbing each other with the sharp edges of their packages. Christmas season was a mean season—fat Santa Clauses ringing their bells in everyone's faces, carols blasting out of loudspeakers, "Let-Us-Adore-Him" and "Christ-the-Lord" in every song. Christmas was a terrible imposition on the Jews. Anna, who had no use for rituals, had made it a special point all her life to ignore Christmas. She left the radio off, didn't venture out, read only the newspaper's front page, which had no ads. Long ago she had told her children, "No presents for me. All I want from you is that you should be happy." Her youngest daughter was a suicide's widow and had health problems; her oldest girl had money troubles. The truth was she should have allowed them to give her store-bought presents. With her fancy rules, they could give her nothing.

Now, two days away from Christmas, she was on her way to the doctor's. All the old people on the bus seemed lame or asthmatic; they were probably all going to the doctor's, and, like her, they were going alone. What could she expect from a world in which a woman of seventy-eight had to take three buses by herself to visit a doctor? At least, in the old days, doctors had made house calls.

An old man was making his way up the aisle, stopping

beside each seat. He swayed beside Anna as if he might land in her lap. He was unshaven and wearing a tattered coat. Thrusting his fist under Anna's nose, he offered her a choice of red-striped candy canes. She turned her head sharply, dismissing him. He had probably put cyanide in them. He bent closer, shaking the cellophane bouquet beside her ear until she locked eyes with him and willed him away.

Well, soon she would be done with Christmases and all the rest of it. How long? She couldn't guess. The years no longer had any definition—one year was like the snap of a finger, no time at all, a mere one seventy-eighth of her life, almost too small a space to count. When she had first learned to play the piano, at seven, a year had been one seventh of her life. To get from her dull Hanon exercises to her first Chopin nocturne had been an eternity of scales, chords, harmony exercises; endless afternoons of winding her metronome and letting its upright brass ticker measure out the practice hours, the beats, the notes that carried her like tiny black birds, away from the raucous life on the lower east side of New York, and later from the wastes of Brooklyn.

Now Anna had trouble with her eyes: the birds waiting on the staff, as if poised on telephone wires, were bunched erratically, blurred together, bumping one another as they waited for her signal. She had trouble with her fingers, too: when the birds began to fly they became lost in black, dense clouds, their delicate shapes concealed, their formations blotted. Her trills, once absolute bells of clarity, sounded now like the rumble of the "el" thundering by when she was a little girl.

A tremendous blast caused Anna to jump halfway out of her seat. A black boy carrying a radio as big as a house had just turned up the volume, and "Silent Night" was coming at her like the open palm of her father's hand. Automatically she pressed her lips together and held her breath.

· · · · ·

Her father was dead sixty years and he could still do this to her! Though he had been out of Poland eight years when she entered the public schools of New York, he had stubbornly forbidden her to sing Christmas carols with the other children. She was allowed only to move her lips during the school's Christmas performances on such phrases as "round yon virgin" and "holy infant." He had instructed her, fiercely, with his hand held up and ready to smack, to weld her lips shut, to be certain that not a flicker of her breath passed through her vocal cords when the forbidden phrase "Christ the Lord" came up. He had been like a madman on the subject, though in most other ways he was a kind and reasonable man.

Anna noticed suddenly that all the old people on the bus were now sucking on red candy canes. They looked like a gathering of lunatics. All of them on their way to their doctors, or to nowhere. Being alive was such a commotion and took so much effort. Why shouldn't they suck on something sweet? What better was there to do?

"So I have a joke for you, Mrs. Goldman," said Dr. Rifkin, her eye doctor, as soon as he walked into the examining room. Silver tinsel hung from the rubber plant against the wall, and the doctor had a little red-and-green Christmas wreath pinned to his white coat. "Four *Yiddishe* mamas get together to play cards." He motioned Anna into the chair where he would tell her how fast she was going blind. He was tall, homely, and overweight. If her daughters had married doctors, they wouldn't be having health problems and money problems.

"The first lady says, '*Oy.*' The second one says, '*Oy vey.*' The third one says, '*Oy vey is mir.*' The fourth one says, "*Ladies, ladies! We promised we wouldn't talk about our children!*'"

Dr. Rifkin laughed loudly at his joke and motioned for Anna to put her chin in the cup. Anna flinched at his deep laughter. She wasn't in that class of women, she resented being thought of as a *Yiddishe* mama and she never played cards.

"So how is life treating you, Mrs. Goldman?" the doctor asked, turning wheels on his machine.

"I don't see well and my fingers don't move where I want them to when I play my Mozart sonatas," she said pointedly.

"Then you're extra lucky to be Jewish. You know why?" he asked, holding the eye dropper right over her head. "You can always play on the keys with your nose!"

64   Anna frowned, letting the numbing drops freeze the surface of her eyes. He darkened the room, and a burning blue light materialized in front of Anna's face. She stared into the heart of it, feeling it burn into her mind. The doctor's head loomed an inch away. Not since Abram's death, except for these visits to Dr. Rifkin, had she felt a man's breath or heard his heavy breathing. When the measurements were taken and the lights turned on—with the doctor again a safe distance away—she steadied herself. It was her opportunity to introduce a new subject.

"Doctor—how often do you think my daughters should have their eyes examined now that I have this condition?" Anna could never ask doctors enough questions, and they never gave her satisfactory answers.

"Oh—once every year or so."

"Not more often?"

"If they want to go more often—sure."

"Shouldn't they go every six months, so if this same problem turns up due to bad heredity, they won't go blind?"

"Mrs. Goldman," said Dr. Rifkin, "what's the difference between a Jewish mother and a vulture?"

"I have no idea," Anna said coldly.

"A vulture only eats hearts after they're dead. A Jewish mother eats her heart out all her life."

• • •

The Christmas tree in the waiting room was broken out in an epidemic of angels; around its fake moss base, empty gift-wrapped boxes were piled. A curly-haired little boy of about four shook each box and then sadly set it down. Anna sat across the room from his parents with her heart pounding. She was to have laser surgery in half an hour. "Your intraocular pressure is way up," Dr. Rifkin had told her. "Not much point in depending on the drops any longer. I'd usually schedule you for another day, but I'm going away for a couple of weeks and we should nip this in the bud. If you can wait till I'm done with my next patient, I'll tell Sally to get things ready, and we'll get this over with. It doesn't hurt, it doesn't take long, you shouldn't have much pain afterward, just a little irritation."

"How do you do it?" Anna had asked. "I've heard it's done without knives, without anesthesia."

"You want me to tell you everything I learned in medical school in two minutes?"

"I just want to know something about what to expect."

"It's magic," said Dr. Rifkin, patting her rudely on the arm. "Don't worry about it. Don't you think I know my stuff?"

The receptionist had asked Anna to sign a release, so if she died it was no one's fault. The procedure was going to cost a thousand dollars. No wonder the doctor could tell jokes all day. She hoped Medicare would pay some of it. In a few minutes she would be taking part in a magic trick. A vulture would be pulled from her heart, pluck out her eyes, and replace in their sockets two cold blue marbles. A man in a black cape would saw her body in half.

"Do you have a candy cane for me?" the little boy said, coming to Anna and putting his hand on her knee.

"Donny, come back here and don't bother the lady. Not everyone gives out candy canes."

"It's okay," Anna said, regretting her suspicions on the bus. "I have grandchildren. I wish I had a candy cane to

give him. He's a sweet boy." Anna wondered what was
wrong with him; glued in the middle of his forehead, like a
great eye, was a silver snap. The boy touched it.

"Don't wrinkle the lady's skirt. Behave yourself," the
boy's mother said. His father added, "Don't touch your
electrode." The parents were young, and looked terrified.
She knew they weren't from Beverly Hills. Anna didn't
dare ask them what she wanted to know. *Is your boy going
blind? Does he have a brain tumor? Something worse?* The
boy had climbed on the couch beside Anna and wiggled his
bottom against the backrest. His hand on her thigh was

66 warm through her skirt. The boy's mother, sitting across
the room with the father, said apologetically, "He probably
thinks you're going to read to him. His grandmother always
reads to him. You look a little like her . . . my mother."

Anna felt the boy's warmth all down her side. His head
brushed against her arm. She could smell his talcum
powder, which reminded her of her own sweet babies, of
that vanished other life. "I have nothing to read to him, but
I can draw him a picture."

"Oh, he'd love that. Donny, come here and give the nice
lady your colored pencils. She'll draw a picture for you."

The boy scrambled off the couch and ran across the room
for the little flat box of pencils and a pad of paper. "I always
come prepared," the mother explained. "We have to wait
for hours sometimes."

"Where are you from?" Anna asked.

"Nevada."

"That's a long way," Anna acknowledged.

"We don't mind coming far," the father said. "We would
go farther. We would go anywhere."

"Wherever the experts are," the mother explained.

"Well, Donny—I only know how to draw one picture."
Anna said. "I'm a one-picture artist. I used to draw a
picture for my little girls. Shall I draw it for you?"

The child nodded his head energetically. The electrode

mirrored the artificial candles flashing on the tree and sent
bursts of red light into Anna's sensitive eyes. She took the
boy's warm little hand and held onto it for a minute.

"Well, now, here we go."

On the tablet she drew in pink the heart-shaped face of a
girl. "Let's call her Wendy," Anna said. With the yellow
pencil, she gave Wendy tight corkscrew curls and wavy
bangs. Her eyelashes, done in black feathery strokes, were
long and demure. Her mouth was a little strawberry rose-
bud.

"What is Wendy doing?" the child asked, looking up at
Anna as she drew little red *x*'s to the edge of the paper.

"She's giving you a hundred kisses," Anna said. "Like
this." She lowered her head and kissed the boy on his
forehead, next to the silver circle. "She wants to be your
sweetheart."

"Thank you," the boy's mother said. "Thank you very
much."

From down the hall, someone called Donny's name.

"Here we go, Donny boy," his father said. Both parents
stood. The father hoisted the boy to his hip.

"Good luck," Anna said. "I wish you all the luck in the
world."

Anna still had the pad and pencils in her lap. She began
to draw a house. It was a child's version of a house, one-
dimensional, with a door and two windows, and a chimney
on the roof which had a spiral of smoke spilling from it into
the sky. Inside was a happy family. She drew the sun and
birds flying. She made the birds into little black notes and
drew telephone wires for them to perch on.

Then, as if by magic, Anna saw the pastel chalk drawing
of a cottage in the country materialize before her eyes. At
the edge of the cottage a stream flowed by under a
weathered wooden bridge. The season was fall, and the
leaves lay in brilliant shifting hills along the road. Dr.

Pincus from Brooklyn was drawing the picture, sitting on
the edge of the bed of Anna's oldest girl, Janet. He had just
told them Janet had pneumonia again. The snowflakes
which had fallen from his coat were melting on the rug at
his feet. Janet had already had her painful injection and
lay limp, tears on her cheeks; every December since she had
started school she had been too sick to attend or take part
in the Christmas play. On this day she seemed to take little
comfort from the doctor's reassuring voice telling her that
her fever would fall, her chest would stop hurting, her
cough would subside. Dr. Pincus had looked around the
room and asked Anna if she wouldn't mind bringing to the
bedside Janet's blackboard, mounted on a rickety easel.
The doctor had stayed there with Janet for a long time,
sitting on the edge of her bed, drawing the landscape very
carefully in pastel chalks: a woodfire sending smoke from
the chimney, a chipmunk on a fencepost, a high and distant
formation of geese honking across the sky. When last of all
he had drawn a graceful young girl with swinging braids—
unmistakably Janet—skipping rope on the wooden bridge,
Janet had laughed weakly, and Dr. Pincus had said, "That's
my girl. That's what I've been waiting to hear."

Janet, that winter, had again missed being in the Christmas play at school, but she had healed. She had lived to
grow up and have money troubles. It was Dr. Pincus who
had urged Anna and Abram to move with their children out
of the bitter winters of New York. Twenty years ago Abram
had died in California of leukemia. Doctor Pincus was
surely dead by now. Doctors had stopped making house
calls, and Anna was about to have her eyes pierced by laser
beams.

"Here's a joke for you," Dr. Rifkin said in the operating
room. "A middle-aged woman comes home from the doctor
and says to her husband, 'The doctor tells me I have
breasts like a twenty-five year old.' The husband answers,

'And what did he say about your fifty-year old ass?' 'Oh,'
says the wife, 'he didn't mention you at all!' ' "

Dr. Rifkin guffawed. Anna sat like a block of ice while the
nurse strapped her head into a contraption.

"Hold your head very still now," the doctor said. "Here
we go."

Meteors flew into Anna's old eyes, deep into her brain,
where she felt her precious memories hiding their faces.
Again and again the doctor fired flaming star showers at
her, in the shapes of her husband and children holding out
their arms to her, and in the forms of quarter notes, eighth
notes, sixteenth notes. She waited for a whole note to come   **69**
flying to her.

"That's it, Mrs. Goldman," the doctor said. "Go home
and no jumping rope this afternoon. Come back in one
week. No—make it two, I'll be in Hawaii. Happy holidays,
and don't worry. Worry never did anyone any good and
never changed the outcome of anything."

"You don't have to tell *me*," Anna said.

When Anna got home, she fell back on her bed in grati-
tude and relief that she was alive and still had her vision.
She turned on the television on her nighttable and saw a
great throng of people looking heavenward, their mouths
wide open, like baby birds about to receive nourishment.
The conductor was on a high podium; the young and the old
in the great auditorium had open songbooks in their hands.
Their faces were aglow as they sang:

> *For unto us a Child is born,*
> *Unto us a Son is given . . .*

The words flashed across the screen as they sang; the eyes
of the singers sparkled with light while the camera moved
slowly from face to face. Anna was about to switch chan-
nels—what did she need this Christmas junk for?—when

the camera stopped and held fast upon the face of a very old woman. She was older than Anna, her features no longer unique, but sunken into a mask of great age. Yet her mouth quivered with passionate energy, and her eyes reflected light as bright as laser beams. Anna sank back on her pillows and attended with half her mind until she heard the soprano sing some words about "the Saviour, which is Christ the Lord."

She stiffened—the same old thing. Anna could feel her father's angry gaze upon her: *Turn that off! Hold your breath. Move only your lips. Don't sing! Clasp your mouth shut! Never say those words!* With an exasperated flap of her hand, Anna held her father off. She felt a flare of fury blaze up in her. She was only interested in the music, didn't he know that? He had bought her her first piano. He had taken her to hear Caruso sing at the Metropolitan Opera house. He, of all people, should know that music was music, and nothing was going to change her at this point in her life.

What fascinated Anna was the evidence of pure happiness which shone on the faces of the singers. There wasn't a mean streak showing anywhere. The camera presented her with an intimate, almost embarrassing, close-up view. She could see pock marks on some faces, little beauty marks and dimples on others. She was much closer than she ever could have been in person—only an inch away from a fat woman; squeezed in with a crowd of young people wearing sweatshirts adorned with the words "Sing Along Messiah"; almost touching a handsome bearded man who looked like Christ Himself. She was right there beside a pregnant woman, brushing arms with a father bending over to point out to his son the correct place in the score—she was with husbands and wives and children, and they were all as happy as Anna had ever seen anyone in her life. The conductor waving his wand was happy. The violinists in the orchestra were smiling as they played, the trumpets shot rainbows of light into the air, the harpsichord strings vi-

. . . . .

brated and caused a shimmering high above in the great vaulted ceiling of the hall. The soprano sang:

Rejoice greatly, O daughter of Zion . . .

Anna, a Jew, was definitely a daughter of Zion. If *she* wasn't, who was? It was too late to discuss this with her father. Anna had lived a long time, and all her life, without question, she had turned her eyes away from the steeples of churches, away from paintings of Jesus in museums, away from gold crosses on the necks of men and women in the street. Anna's eyes burned as she studied the rapt singers. She listened, unthreatened, with the ears of her natural skepticism:

Then shall the eyes of the blind be opened, and the ears of the deaf unstopped, then shall the lame man leap as an hart, and the tongue of the dumb shall sing.

Suddenly slapping her bed with the palm of her hand, Anna addressed her father: *Papa, listen to the music!* Something was causing happiness to shine on those faces. Something made that old man on the bus give out his candy canes, made Dr. Rifkin, for all his joking, sit there behind his magic machine-gun to do what he could do to keep Anna seeing the world. Someone had invented that one-eyed silver electrode to shine in the middle of Donny's forehead.

Anna felt, without doubt, that every one of the singers was beautiful. It was not like her, it was not her way. Normally she would have made private notations to herself about this one's fake blonde hair with dark roots showing, or that one's bad skin, or the morals of the careless young that the world turned out these days—those braless sloppy girls and the boys with green hair and gold studs in their ears. Old women with scarves around their turkey-skin necks could never fool her. She always had ready, in neat

. . . . .

bars of music, a song of many ungenerous verses waiting to be sung. But the music in her head had modulated. She wondered if the surgery had changed her vision in some profound way. She felt like putting her arms around each person in the singing throng—the scarred, the fat, the heavily made-up, the too pretty to be true. When the chorus sang:

Surely he hath borne our griefs . . .

Anna thought she would buy her daughters presents. Maybe she would ask them to buy *her* a present. What did she want? A record of Handel's *Messiah*? Her father had his hand up, ready to hit. *Leave me alone!* she told him. *So what if I don't hold my breath when those words come around! You've made a big mistake. You worry too much.*

She felt funny, a little like laughing. A little like singing. She wasn't much of a laugher or a singer. She hadn't sung in perhaps seventy years. But she lived alone in a little apartment—who was going to judge her? Sitting up straight in her bed, she smoothed back her hair as if she were about to take her place in the crowd and be shown on television, her eyes twinkling with light. Nervously, she began to sing along as the words appeared on the screen. It took a while for her to get used to the sound of her own thin, wavering voice rising in her darkened bedroom, but soon she gained volume and strength, and finally, with confidence, she brought herself in tune with the others.

TICKETS TO
DONAHUE
. . . .

A truck driver with an extremely important mustache
(also with muscles like braids poking out the sleeves of his T-
shirt) stared straight at Anna, dared her with his eyes to
keep staring at him. He sat high in his shiny red rig and, for
an instant, when he turned his head around to reach for a
cigarette, she could see the points of his mustache sticking
out from behind his ears. He'd parked his truck directly in
front of the NBC Studios on Alameda Street, leaving it
there to belch diesel fumes into Anna and Gert's faces while
they stood on line for the *Donahue* show. He showed no
signs of moving on. Anna knew his breed—the kind of man
who tried to stare you down, who thought if he tried long
enough he could get you to think the way he was thinking.
She'd worked on Wall Street in the thirties and had enough
of those stares from men on subway platforms who were
forever trying to get a look at her ankles.

Anna noticed with satisfaction that Gert was watching the
way the truckdriver was staring at her. Men had always
been after Anna (her ankles were still elegant), and Gert
had always been shocked. Gert didn't understand the
power of sex. To this day she bragged about having been a
virgin at thirty-nine when she married the first of her two
old husbands. A sister so backward was an embarrassment
to Anna. Barney had bowled Gert over with a few bouquets
of wilted flowers stolen from a neighbor's garden. Anna had
tried to set Gert straight; she had known at once Barney

was an opportunist, a taker. He had children he was going to look out for first—all he wanted from Gert was someone to cook his dinners and iron his shirts. Anna understood human nature, but Gert was willing to be fooled. She had prayed for a trousseau all her life, and for one red lace nightgown she was willing to take on a man who, as part of the agreement, insisted on dragging his teenaged daughter to live with them. This was a girl who slept, snoring, on a cot in the living room. This was a girl who ate sardines with her fingers. Even when Gert learned (from Anna, who had done plenty of detective work) that Barney was giving most of his company's profits to his sons and crying poor to Gert, Gert was willing to forgive him. The sons had families, she explained to Anna—they *needed* more.

74

That was the kind of fool she was. Anna wondered how she and Gert had ever come to be sisters, born in the same family, from the same mother and father, in the same house, only two years apart. Even now—as the two of them stood reflected in the truck's gleaming side—their resemblance ended with their white hair. Gert was dolled up in a ruffled pink-flowered dress and wearing a necklace of arthritic coral sticks, which were jabbing her neck, while Anna wore a simple tailored beige blouse and brown skirt. Gert liked to wear a lot of makeup, and Anna wore none. They looked accidentally thrown together: a hillbilly and a woman from a list of the year's Ten Best Dressed. Anna noticed her frown reflected in the truck's side and immediately let her face relax. Their mother used to threaten them with dire results: one day their ugly expressions would freeze that way forever. Gert had always taken the warning seriously— she kept a cow-like smile on her face. If she saw babies, old ladies, dogs in the street, she'd greet them with soft, sympathetic cow eyes. She'd never figured out that babies grew up to be like anyone else who robbed you, but a person couldn't explain such things to Gert. Gert was the original Pollyanna.

. . . . .

The stink from the cloud of black exhaust was getting to be too much. Anna caught the eye of the driver and coughed. He lifted his pinky and twirled his mustache. She swung her head the other way. She'd leave the line this minute if it wouldn't mean losing their places—pressed as they were against a wooden fence with hundreds of other people waiting to get inside to see the show.

"Stop looking at him like that," Gert said, poking Anna in the side.

"Like what?"

"With your glamor-girl look," Gert said.

"You're crazy," Anna said.

"You just tossed your hair. Someday you won't get away with that. Men used to follow you home from the subway for that look. So don't act so innocent. That look of yours fooled Abram into marrying you, and then you made him beg for love all his life."

"You're crazy," Anna said, and then a rock of fear crept into her mind. "What do you mean?"

"Nothing," Gert said. She adjusted her eyeglasses on their fake pearl chain. "You know—if it hadn't been for me Abram never would have had his rightful rewards . . ."

"What rightful rewards?"

"You know what I mean, his wedding night rights."

Anna felt a momentary dizziness. Gert *was* crazy. The fumes were whirling around her head—she swayed and leaned back against the wall of the building.

"What's the matter?"

"It's that stink."

"Cover your nose right away with your handkerchief, Anna. Norman Cousins breathed in fumes from an airplane and he got a fatal disease."

"It wasn't fatal," Anna corrected her. "He cured it by laughing at old movies."

"If *you* got it, it would be fatal," Gert warned her. "You never laugh at low humor, so don't imagine you could start now. I remember when you were a girl you got nauseous from Groucho Marx, from Jack Benny, even from Eddie Cantor. So cover your nose."

"It's impossible that I got nauseous from Groucho Marx," Anna said. ". . . and the word is *nauseated*. I never could bear him, the man disgusted me."

"Exactly," Gert agreed. "You were always too good for everything."

"Why do you make things up?" Anna demanded. "You're always telling me things from the old days that never happened."

76 "They happened," Gert said. "It's just convenient for you not to remember."

"I never tell *you* ridiculous things about yourself!" Anna said.

"That's right—you never paid attention to me, you never gave me a thought. You were too busy looking in the mirror, combing your crowning glory."

"I thought it was Ava who never paid attention to you."

"She's another sister for the books. When it comes to sisters God wasn't good to me. I always wished we could be like the Andrews Sisters. But at least I don't have to deal with Ava now—let her stay in Miami Beach till the cows come home."

"Let's not get into how much you hate Ava," Anna said, "or I'll be sorry I invited you along."

"I'm sorry I came already," Gert said.

The truck blurped three shots of black smoke into the air and tooted its horn. Anna looked up. The driver leaned forward toward the windshield and made a fish-mouth kiss at Anna as he pulled away from the curb.

"Disgusting," Gert said as they watched his tail end merge into traffic. "The world is a sewer these days. Whatever happened to parties and wholesome hayrides?"

"Hayrides!" Anna echoed.

"You can be sure what kind of guest Donahue's having on today," Gert went on.

.　.　.　.　.

"What kind?" Anna asked.

"A sex guest," Gert said. "Donahue always has sex on his show."

"I thought you never watch Donahue."

"I click by him fast on the dial."

"Look," Anna said, "since sex is a fact of life, since you're a woman who's had two husbands by now, why can't you finally face it? If you paid a little attention to what's going on in the world these days, you might come out of the fog of the old days and learn something."

"You should talk! You're the one who doesn't have any understanding of these things. You don't have animal appetites, Anna. You were born with some kind of cotton stuffing inside you instead of flesh."

"*I* was! What about you, the famous virgin at thirtynine?"

"You weren't a virgin on your wedding night?"

"Of course I was. But I was young! I was still a girl!"

"I know some girls who aren't virgins," Gert said ominously.

"Who?"

"Your granddaughters," Gert said.

"What have *they* got to do with anything? What do you know about them anyway? They don't tell me about their private lives! I'm sure they don't tell *you!* They probably don't even tell their mother!"

"They're college girls," Gert said, "and I know what college girls are up to these days. They live in co-ed dorms. They share the same bathrooms with men!"

"You know everything, don't you?" Anna said in disgust. "If you listened to Donahue like I do, you'd be more understanding of the way the world is today. You could learn something."

"I've watched enough to know exactly what I would learn! I could learn how to be a lesbian and have a baby with my lesbian lover's brother, so we can all be one big happy family."

. . . . .

"Oh, get your head out of the Middle Ages," Anna said in disgust. "This is almost the year 2000."

"I'm glad Papa didn't live long enough to see what's become of the world."

"You think Papa was so innocent?" Anna said. "When he married Mama, what do you think he was marrying? Her brains?"

"Bite your tongue," Gert said. "Papa was a religious man."

"He was a *man*," Anna said.

"So was Abram a man," Gert said. "Or didn't you ever notice? You think Abram only wanted to pray on his wedding night?"

Anna tried to remember her wedding night. Could such a thing be possible—for a woman to forget her wedding night? "Thank heaven—" she said, "this line is beginning to move." She gave Gert a little shove. "Will you walk?" she said impatiently. "I want to get in there before they fill up."

The line suddenly began to shoot forward. A young woman carrying a walkie-talkie and wearing an NBC peacock emblem on her jacket pocket ran along beside them and herded them into a vast ceilingless cavern. It was like the dark inside of a refrigerator. She rushed them over cables and wires taped to the floor, she sent them up wide flat stairs to find seats.

"Be sure to take an aisle seat," Gert advised Anna, "or he won't be able to get to you."

"What makes you think I care if he gets to me?" Anna asked.

"Because you always have to be the center of attention," Gert said. "But don't bother to toss your hair for him," Gert added. "Your charms had their day, Anna, but face it—their day is over."

Donahue's guest was a young woman who looked like a school teacher but was really a whorehouse madam. Her ancestors had come over on the Mayflower. She was dressed like a girl going to church. Pretty, blonde, and blue-eyed, she sat on a chair and folded her hands in her lap. Her dress resembled a kind of middy-blouse Anna used to wear as a child. A string of white pearls lay on her throat. Anna observed how respectful Phil Donahue was to her; she disapproved. Why should a man as educated and intelligent as Donahue have to knock himself out for a woman like that—running around the audience with his coattails flying and his microphone sticking forward like a giant mushroom.

They were talking about the madam's business—how her "girls" were very smart and cultured, that many were college students, one was even a medical student. What other jobs could they find, she said, that had such good hours and such high pay? She provided regular medical care for them. Her girls carried little charge-card machines in their purses. They carried extra pantyhose and business clothes for the next day. They were refined, intelligent women, just women earning a decent living.

The floodlights, burning brightly now and heating up the room rapidly, seemed aimed at Anna's face. She squinted in the glare. Donahue went on smiling and nodding as if the whorehouse business was just fine with him; the trouble with liberals was that they forgave everyone for everything.

Gert poked Anna.

"Does anyone know what kind of part-time jobs your granddaughters have at college?" she demanded. "Do you think Janet knows what her children do?"

"You're crazy," Anna said. "My granddaughters are not prostitutes."

"Do you know for sure where they sleep every night?"

"No!" Anna said. "Do you know for sure where *I* sleep every night?"

"I have no doubts about you," Gert said. "You aren't the type to sleep around. You only like to tease."

. . . . .

Anna was feeling dizzy. She was the older sister, she had always believed she understood everything better than Gert. Now her head was reeling. All these questions raised about her granddaughters, about her wedding night! Was she a tease because she liked to wear her skirts short? She had always had pretty legs, why shouldn't she? She saw in her mind the red truck, the spurting black smoke, the truckdriver throwing her a kiss.

"Let's leave," Anna said. "This show is worthless."

"I'm more than willing," Gert said. "For this I had to waste a taxi coupon."

"Look," Anna said, "Donahue could have had on Ralph Nader talking about poison in hair dye. He could have had on someone from the PLO. He didn't send me a program. He's only in LA for a week and this is what we got."

"We got sewage! From the sewer of the world!" Gert said. She waved her arm to dismiss the whole thing, and suddenly Donahue came bounding up the steps with his microphone quivering in front of him and grabbed Gert's arm. He leaned right across Anna. He was so close she could see the thin white stripes on his pinstripe suit, the glare of the spotlights on his wedding ring. The hairs on his hand holding the microphone were glowing like hot electric wires.

"C'mon, help me out here!" he said to Gert as he thrust the black knob toward her mouth, bending toward her as if he cared with all his heart exactly what Gert thought about every issue in life. He took her hand and pulled her gently to a standing position. "Tell us what you think." He had a voice like a lover.

"What I think," Gert said, "is with all the troubles in the world, who needs to put a woman like this on national television!"

A round of applause rose up all around them. The Mayflower Madam smiled sweetly and cast her eyes down; the applause for Gert was deafening. Donahue smiled at Gert and squeezed her hand. Anna could smell his cologne or his

. . . . .

aftershave or something from his beautiful white hair. She
was the one who had got the free tickets, and Gert was the
one who had got to air her small-mindedness all over the
United States of America.

Anna raised her hand, but Donahue's back was to her, he
was rushing down the stairs—her chance was lost forever.
She turned to Gert and saw how flushed her cheeks were. A
smile as big as a freeway was on her face.

"He's a real *mensch*," Gert said. "I could go for him."

"I thought he was too liberal for you."

"He's only that way on television. In real life he's married
to a good Catholic girl," Gert said. "He knows what's right.
He's a good family man. I would be happy for my daughters
to marry a man like that."

"You have no daughters," Anna said. "You have no children, and it's lucky for them you don't."

"I wonder if my friends in New Jersey saw me," Gert said
as they waited at the curb for a taxi. She had insisted on
staying till the very end of the show, and then rushed to join
the crush of women as they filed forward to shake Donahue's hand.

"No doubt they saw you all over the continent. Probably
the President of the United States heard you, too."

"I hope so. He would agree with my opinion," Gert said.
"He and I have the same politics."

"What do you know about politics?" Anna said. "All you
ever read is 'Dear Abby.'"

"I know the world used to be a better place. That's all I
need to know."

"Oh!" Anna said. *"Why don't you grow up?"*

"You think it's grown up to cry for an hour in the
bathroom on your wedding night?" Gert said. "Sitting on
the tile in a brown silk dress and bawling your head off?"

"That's nonsense," Anna said. "I never cry. I didn't cry
then and I don't cry now."

"You were afraid to be left alone for the night with Abram."

"Not true."

"He came to me and begged me to calm you down. He had a hotel room reserved in Atlantic City, but you didn't want to go away from home after the ceremony. You were hysterical."

"Ridiculous."

"He thought maybe I could arrange it so you and he could spend the first night alone at our house, then you wouldn't be so scared. What I had to go through!"

82 "What did you have to go through?" Anna asked. She couldn't remember a single thing about her wedding except the violent odor of her corsage of gardenias, curling brown at the edges almost as soon as she got them.

"First I had to get Mama farmed out. The Bronx relatives finally agreed to take her home with them and bring her back the next day. Then I had to find a place for myself. Do you know where I had to sleep on your wedding night?"

"No," Anna said coldly. "The way you adored Abram, maybe it was with him. How should I know what else you're making up in this crazy story?"

"He really should have married me," Gert said. "I have a sweeter nature than you. He would have had a better life with me. The fact is, Rosie Dubin and her husband had just taken an apartment on Ocean Parkway, and they agreed to let me come and sleep there after the ceremony. But they had only one double bed. So I had to sleep in it with them. They made me get in the middle, between them, to prove there wouldn't be any hanky-panky to embarrass me."

"It must have been a big night for you, the famous virgin, sleeping in a bed with a man."

"We laughed all night," Gert said, smiling. A big bus blasted past them, and her hair blew back in the wind. She looked almost young and pretty.

"Late as I married, I always enjoyed sex, Anna. Did you?"

. . . . .

"When Donahue has me on as his guest, I'll discuss it in public, not before."

The taxi they'd ordered pulled up, and Gert held the door open as Anna got in. As hard as Anna tried, she could not remember her wedding, her wedding night, her honeymoon. Had she ever enjoyed sex? What a question. She could hardly remember sex. When it happened, it was in the dark, late at night, she was always tired, she kept her eyes closed. Abram never stayed there long, he didn't bother her too often. What was to enjoy? Did Gert know something she didn't know? Did her granddaughters? All her life she had considered herself so advanced, but could it be she was the one still in the Dark Ages?

The taxi driver, a handsome Armenian, drove them toward home. He had some music playing on the radio with a low, hard beat. He seemed to be in another world. On Santa Monica Boulevard they passed a porno movie. They passed young girls strutting about in short shorts. They saw two gay men looking in the window of an underwear store, their arms around each other's waists. They passed a billboard with a half-naked woman in a bikini, advertising an airline. Gert had a satisfied expression on her face. Anna suddenly grabbed her arm. "I slept in the same bed with Abram thirty-one years, Gert. I had two babies. Doesn't that prove something to you?"

"What does it prove? Who knows which way you were facing?" She took a red lipstick out of her purse and rolled it around her lips without looking in a mirror. She squeezed her lips together. "You know, I had two husbands already," Gert said. "If this one doesn't hold out, I'll find another one. If necessary, I'll have three, maybe four."

"You're seventy-six years old," Anna said. "You must be crazy."

"So I'm crazy," Gert said. "You should be so crazy. Here, put on some nice bright lipstick and enjoy your life a little, Anna."

THE NEXT MEAL
IS *LUNCH*

. . . .

One of the gay boys across the alley was hucking and hocking in his bathroom, which looked directly into Anna's kitchen window. She pushed away her dish of cottage cheese—how could a person be expected to eat when these poor boys were dying like flies all over the place? And where were their mothers on a special day like this? If one of her daughters had AIDS, Anna would be right there, holding the bowl for her to throw up in, especially on Thanksgiving, when no one should be alone.

She was alone. Accidentally, of course. A big dinner had been planned, as usual, at her daughter Janet's, with Carol making the stuffing and Gert and Harry bringing the canned sweet potatoes. But then Janet had come down with the flu. Anna certainly hoped it was the flu, but these days who could know? She had always thought her son-in-law was perfectly respectable, but from the talk shows Anna knew that almost anyone you met could be a closet bisexual or have a file cabinet full of heroin.

Today was a hard day to be alone. It happened Anna's birthday came this year on Thanksgiving Day, and this one was not chicken feed, this was eighty, this was the Big Time. She'd already been planning how she would break up and distribute the chocolate turkey her daughters always gave her. The hollow head, she'd decided, would go to her youngest granddaughter, who had won a ten-thousand-dol-

. . . . .

lar scholarship to college and proved to Anna—not that she needed proof—the superiority of her genes.

She heard the sick boy cough again, half-choking, half-strangling. Could the AIDS virus leap across an alley? On the news they talked all the time about safe sex! When was sex ever safe? At its best it gave you children, and some children (of course not hers!) could ruin your life as fast as any fatal disease. Thank God Anna was past *that* minefield—no chance of getting pregnant and no chance of having rotten children. Now all she had to worry about was the diseases of old age. When she went, she wanted to go fast. And if she had the bad luck to linger, she only hoped someone would make short work of her.

It crossed her mind she should cook chicken soup for the gay boy and bring it in to him, but, as usual, whenever she had a generous impulse, her good sense ruled it out. Neither did she want to hang around here and listen to him *krekhts* all day.

"So I'm going for a walk," she announced to her furniture, to her two pianos, to the ghosts who hopped around her apartment. "I should only live to see you again, I shouldn't be mugged." This was said to protect her from the evil eye though Anna had no use for those old and meaningless superstitions. Still, if a person anticipated all the terrible conclusions, they couldn't sneak up on you. She didn't take a purse—a strategy designed to discourage muggers, and she took her ID in her sweater pocket, in case she got hit by a truck.

A truck hit Anna the minute she stepped off the curb at Melrose and Fairfax. For the first time in her life she flew like a bird, but grunting. And hit down like a rock, but bursting. Blood was in her mouth. She saw a Mexican jump out of the truck and felt him take her gently under the arms and drag her back on the sidewalk. She was sorry she had ever wished they would all go back to Mexico. He was staring into her eyes with a passion she couldn't identify, but it moved her. She wished he were her son. Daughters could be devious (she was lucky hers were not!) while sons usually adored their mothers. She was about to ask him if he was good to his mother when he stamped his foot.

"Lady! You crazy? You must be blind!" He pinched her arm. "Give me *money*. You make me late for work!"

He growled over her with a dog's mouth, menacing her, his mustache curved like a scythe. Anna felt a veil descend over her eyes.

"Shit, man," he said. "Shit, you losing me my job, man." He kicked at her thigh. She saw him climb back into his truck and roar away.

"Give me money," she mumbled as she lowered her head down to the pavement. "Give me money. That's all anyone knows these days."

THE DAY IS *THURSDAY*
THE CITY IS *NECTAR HILL*
THE WEATHER IS *CLOUDY*
THE NEXT MEAL IS *LUNCH*

The sign hung on the wall directly in front of Anna's bed. Anna privately added a fifth line:

THE PERSON FORCED TO READ THIS IS A *MORON*.

She had lain here during the risings and settings of several suns, but the day remained Thursday, the next meal always lunch. She was strapped into her bed; at intervals she was turned like a frankfurter on a barbecue grill. A pattern of motion occurred around her: white-coated forms circled in the hall. Nurses slid along on their rubber shoes, carrying Dixie cups filled with little pills; aides, with their sullen faces, threw down lunchtrays, refilled water pitchers. An old woman in a red furry robe pushed her wheel-

chair up and down the corridor, crying: "They poison my
food. My son stole my house. What comes out in the toilet is
black. No one believes me." In the background an old man
crooned, "Nonno, nonno," never stopping, never changing
his tone.

The moment Anna's daughters materialized at her bedside, she said, "Get me out of here." She saw them look at
one another. "Listen," she said. "The weather isn't cloudy,
the next meal isn't lunch, and I'm not a vegetable. Not yet."
She motioned to the other two beds in her room, sporting
horrors she preferred not to memorize. "You can't get lox
and bagels here. What does it cost me to stay here a day?"

Her girls gave each other another look. They'd already
explained to Anna that the hospital to which the ambulance
had taken her refused to keep her because she wasn't badly
hurt, so until her dizziness went away she had to stay here
in this nursing home. She'd told them she wasn't dizzier
than usual and she wasn't ready for a nursing home. Now a
panic rose in her lower belly, along with a premonition of
her future here, a place from which she couldn't call her
congressman, or write a letter to the newspaper, or threaten
anyone with a lawsuit. Unable to escape, she would be
reduced to a lump of nothing.

She thought of her miserable apartment with longing; it
now seemed as spacious and fragrant as Yosemite itself, her
narrow stall shower a waterfall, her white stove vent a snow-
capped mountain. Never mind the Armenians' barbecue
fumes, never mind the germs coming across the alley from
the gay boy. A haven of freedom was what her apartment
was—where no one told her what day, what weather, what
town she was forced to endure in. Was it possible she would
never get back there?

In a drawer by her bed at home she had her Hemlock
Society card; if her daughters didn't get her out of here, she
would phone the society and ask for the name of some

doctor in Holland who could mail her the correct pills as
soon as possible. Was it a major problem that her children
would be insulted when they realized they weren't important enough to keep her alive? She began to compose a note
to them: *"Believe me, children, this has nothing to do with
the way you treated me and it's not that life wasn't worth
living, especially with your father (I wish I believed I
would meet him and be his footstool in heaven, but dead in
my opinion is dead, what can I tell you?) and it's not that
my grandchildren aren't dear to me, but look, let's face it,
they're not interested in me—do they ever come to visit?"*
This last she decided to leave out—she didn't need to create
any extra hostility. *Please be advised I'm no coward—
you'll find out some day that old age isn't for sissies.*

She began to imagine her funeral: what she wanted was
for the girls to play a tape of herself performing Mozart on
the piano; maybe a little Chopin, a page or two of the
"Pathétique," a little "Claire de Lune"—a sampling of her
well-rounded repertoire. Maybe even "The You and I
Waltz," the first piece she had ever learned by heart.

But definitely no fancy ceremonies. Certainly no rabbis,
those crooks. No strangers either, just a tasteful gathering
to the tune of great music, played by Anna's gifted but
deceased fingers.

She sensed a breeze passing over her face and saw some
papers flutter in front of her eyes.

"Ma?" she heard. She blinked.

"Janet and I have some papers we think you should sign."
A thin tube—a pen—was slid into her hand, a hard surface
appeared beneath her forearm. They unstrapped her
straps.

"What papers?" she said.

"We think you need to let us handle your money from
now on, Ma," Janet said. "If you give us your money—then
after two years the government will pay for your bills here."

· · · · ·

"*Two years?*" Anna yelled. "You think I'm going to stay in this zoo for two years? You're crazy!"

"A lawyer advised us to do this, Ma. It's perfectly legal. It's just a protection."

"You're seeing lawyers about my money?" Anna said. "Who are you protecting?"

She knew the look they were giving each other, it was the look you give over the head of a crazy person.

"What're you doing, Ma?"

Anna rolled out of bed and landed with a clunk on the floor. The stroke victim in the next bed peered down at her and began to hum.

"Listen," Anna said, on her hands and knees, "a Brownie troop is coming tomorrow to bring candy canes. The aides are putting up a Christmas tree in the hall. A chaplain is coming to pray with us and remind us of the suffering of Jesus. You want me to be here for *that?* I'm still your mother, children," she said fiercely, "so get me out of this joint right now."

At Carol's house they argued with her all night. They wanted her to give up her apartment. The time had come. All right, she was a reasonable woman. She could see the sense of some of their arguments: it was dangerous to live alone, hard to shop, she never liked to cook much anyway. In a retirement home she'd have better nourishment, security, care, protection, and, if she fell, help on the spot. The two of them would take care of everything, move her to a place nearby, they'd visit her all the time. (No one said anything about her living with them, but, fine, she was a modern old woman, she knew children didn't take you in anymore.)

"You wouldn't have to visit me all the time, believe me."

"So you'll agree to move?"

"I'm helpless in the hands of fate," Anna said. What can I do?"

90

．．．．．

She moved her two pianos with her; it wasn't easy fitting them into her room, but Anna was gratified to see it made quite an impression on the staff of the Country Gardens Retirement Home, how their mouths dropped open when the elevator groaned under the weight of her instruments, one baby grand, one upright. In her room, she directed the movers to set her bed between the two of them so that she could reach up with either hand and find a keyboard waiting for her.

"So children: this is the last stop," she said lugubriously for her daughters' benefit as the three of them signed registration papers at the desk in the lobby, but she was noticing a bunch of old ladies watching her, ladies with legs like elephants, ladies with eyeglasses like Pyrex plates. She saw a couple of old men, too; nothing to get excited about, stooped over, with walkers, with canes, but she had a feeling it wasn't going to be so bad as she thought. Who knew what energy she still had in her? When had she last had a chance to try out her popularity?

At the end of her first week, one of the old ladies got hold of Anna and said, "Unkind things are being said about you in the dining hall, my dear. Bend lower and I'll tell you." They were examining the menu for the week, tacked on the bulletin board.

"I might slip a disc if I bend down," Anna said. She was very careful now, with the threat of the nursing home in her mind. "Just talk louder."

"You've *got* to wear your skirts longer," the woman whispered to her. "I'm telling you this for your own good. It isn't your fault you have such pretty legs."

"What should I do, cut them off?" Anna asked. The menu in front of them was unbelievable: crab quiche, Louisiana frogs' legs, chimichanga, chile relleno. At moments like this, Anna wished she had not dismissed so viciously the Jewish Home for the Aged. There at least they would occasionally have potato latkes, blintzes, kreplach.

"Also, certain people have noticed, I won't say who, that you don't wear earrings. You don't curl your hair."

"So tell them not to look," Anna said. "Tell them I believe in natural beauty."

"And one more thing we think you should know: stay away from the man in the brown plaid shirt. He has only one thing on his mind—sex."

"Believe me," Anna said, "I wouldn't go near the King of England if he had sex on his mind."

The joke going around was that everyone at Country Gardens had AIDS; "Guess what kind of AIDS I have?" "You have AIDS?" "Yeah—hearing aids." Or: "Guess what disease I have?" "What disease?" "Oldtimer's Disease." If it made them happy to be comedians, let them be comedians, like the old lady who came down to dinner one night wearing a Groucho Marx nose. Anna hadn't liked vulgarity as a young woman, and she didn't like it now. Thank heaven she hadn't got coarse with age. Mozart and Culture were her creeds—she'd tell the old ladies to put that in their pipes and smoke it the next time someone asked her what church she attended on Sundays. Or she'd answer that her religion was Beauty, that she got spiritual insights from Rachmaninoff. What else could she say to all those clanking pearl earrings hanging between scrolls of blue-white hair and flowered polyester dresses; how did you defend against a little army of Church Ladies?

Anna wore what was left in her closet from the old days—graceful pleated skirts, sheer stockings, high heels (these she had to wear because of a spur on her instep), and a tailored blouse with a roadrunner pin (a gift from Abram) on the collar. She weighed a hundred pounds; the other old ladies weighed two hundred. She saw them looking at her

. . . . .

calves, at her short skirts, and she swung her hips more grandly as she walked down the carpeted halls.

The shape of Anna's days had changed—at home she had had no structure: a walk to Fairfax was her outing, or she could lie there all day like a dog. But here they had everything: an exercycle room (a nurse right next-door), a beauty shop, a library, a crafts room, a bingo room, a banking room where once a week you could cash checks. A maid came and gave you clean towels and sheets. How could she afford this? The fact was she had no money at all anymore; her girls had stripped her of every cent in the interest of some future good. They were paying her bills, and they told her to put money worries out of her mind. If she couldn't trust her children, who could she trust? Her life of responsibility was over. She was free as a bird.

Coming toward the dining hall she smelled the luscious odor of frying onions (the thought of onions alone used to make her sick; now her mouth watered). She felt as if this were the college she had never attended, the dormitory life she had never had. Heads turned when she came into the dining hall; if she could still see to thread a needle, she'd sew the hems on all her skirts and make them even shorter.

Of course, when her daughters called her, she complained; the food was awful, the heater didn't work, there were roaches in the bathroom—and when they came to visit, she let her knees buckle, she told them she had headaches, that her sciatica was back, her osteoporosis was going wild. The instant they were gone, she went downstairs and climbed on the exercycle and did a mile.

The man in the brown plaid shirt took a seat across from her at dinner. "I'm Harvey and I'm eighty-six," he said. "I understand you have two pianos. Fancy that. I have two cellos."

"I don't do duets," Anna said.

"I can see you're a smart cookie," he said. "I can see

you've been around. Now me," he said, "I am a famous architect. I built 280 houses in the San Gabriel Hills alone. I can prove it." He reached into his pocket and handed her a photocopy of an article, telling how famous he was.

"I'm not impressed," Anna said, handing it back. "At this point in my life, only Arthur Rubinstein could impress me."

"I have it over him," the man said. "I'm still alive."

"Maybe, but only barely," Anna observed. She ordered her dinner from the waitress. "Easy on the onions," she said. "I might have a date later on."

That night Harvey-plaid-shirt knocked on the door of her room. When she opened the door, he pulled a gun on her.

"Stick 'em up," he said. Then he pulled the trigger. A flag that said "BANG!" fell from the barrel.

"They told me you were a sex maniac," Anna said. "You go around armed, too?"

"Only when I meet my match," he said. "And I think I have, kid, with you."

"You certainly are conceited," Anna told him.

"See what I mean?" he said. "I met my match. You and I are a pair, kid. We're survivors. You don't get to our age unless you're smart, tough, and lucky."

Just then the phone rang. Anna's sister Gert said: "How come you weren't in your room last night?"

"I had Bingo."

"A gambler you're becoming in your old age?"

"Don't worry," Anna said. "I use plenty of self-control."

"And the night before?" Gert asked.

"I was at Potpourri. We have an entertainment night. I was playing the piano for my friends."

"What's this with the nightlife?" Gert asked. "And what kind of friends? You never made a friend in your life."

"You sound a little jealous," Anna said. "Someday, after Harry dies, you can move in here. You'll see for yourself."

. . . . .

"Don't tell me you like it there!"

Harvey was aiming his gun at her again.

"Don't aim for the eyes," she warned him.

"You have someone there?" Gert asked.

"A friend, he just stopped by for a minute."

"A man in your room already! And you sound cheerful,"
Gert accused her. "A week ago you told me this is the last
stop!" Gert said. "In your own words you said so. 'I hope I
die in my sleep,' you said."

"Now I see it could be a long last stop," Anna said. "It
could be a vacation."

Harvey fired his pistol.

Anna laughed. She had the clear impression she was
getting younger.

WHEEL OF FORTUNE
. . . .

Twice a week, maybe more, Anna saw the aides from her wing run up and down the hall of the nursing home closing the doors to the corridor. Anna was not so dumb, but she played dumb—she liked to see what excuses they came up with. "Why are you doing that?" she cried out, clarifying her right to have her door open, that it was her business if she wanted to see the riffraff passing in the halls or have a little diseased air circulating around her bed.

Usually they answered: "We're cleaning the hall." Sometimes they confessed something closer to the truth: "We have an emergency"—and whap, the door was closed and no further conversation was possible. Once they even told her they were spraying for bugs.

Today the young Mexican aide seemed stumped, paused in her rush to pull the door closed. "A rat is loose," she said finally (but her eyes showed the guilt of lying). All the Mexicans who worked here were Catholic and worried constantly about sin. One of Anna's male aides told her as he changed her sheets one day that he envied her because her sinning days were over.

For a brief moment Anna believed there *might* be a rat at large. A rat! *That* would be an interesting change from the daily visitors who popped their heads into her room without invitation: the lady with the cart of toys (she passed out sheets torn from a child's coloring book and some knobby crayons for those who still had motor control of their hands), the lady who carried her pet poodle from room to room, urging the inmates to pet the dog because the elderly, as Anna had heard her tell a nurse in the hall, needed "sensory nourishment and the comfort of touch." But that was no rat they had closed the door against just now—that was a dead body rolling past. Anna envied the lucky duck who had the good fortune to have the arrow (she was thinking of the *Wheel of Fortune*) land on her. Though, given the odds, it was probably a *him*. Men seemed to have more luck in every way.

Wheel of Fortune was the only TV show Anna permitted herself to watch. (All the others were designed for idiots.) Anna happened to be a word wizard—she always got every question right before the contestants did—even the champions. Furthermore, the show supported her certainty that luck was everything—the questions you got, where the arrow landed, who was spinning the wheel—the kind of urgent factors over which a person had no control, whether it was on TV or in real life or in the gambling casino.

Anna's daughter Janet had recently gone to Las Vegas and brought Anna a picture of the three sevens that won her a jackpot on a slot machine. The snapshot was pasted up on Anna's wall now (777 on the center line), although Janet had said it was illegal to take pictures in a casino, and she could have been thrown out for doing it. She just wanted, she said, to prove to herself she had been lucky at some point in her life.

Had Anna been lucky? She could have died young, like her husband. She could have been a famous pianist, like Horowitz, like Rubinstein, only she was born a woman (another accident of where the arrow landed). She could have been born into a better, richer, smarter family, not having had a peasant for a mother and a sickly tailor (with a love for Caruso) for a father. She could have married a lawyer, a doctor . . . oh what was the use of it?

Even here at the nursing home, accidents of fate were

everything. Which roommate you got, which aide was as-
signed to give you a shower, which cut of horse-meat they
gave you for dinner. Luckily, Anna's esophagus had
clamped shut after her series of misfortunes: her stroke,
her fall, her emergency hip surgery and all its complications (pulmonary blood clots, pneumonia, heart arrhyth-
mia, but nothing worthwhile enough to kill her). Due to
that particular stroke of luck (who had the strength to chew
after all that?), she chose to excuse herself from eating for
the rest of her existence.

Various visitors who stopped in to see her appeared
shocked when they noticed the pulsating snake of her clear **99**
plastic feeding tube, pumping a malted of nutrients that
disappeared under the covers and went into a hole in her
belly. These were people still under the delusion that eating
was one of life's pleasures. Anna had long ago passed beyond wanting to deal with gristle, fat, egg-white slime, or
the seeds of small berries. Quite a few burdens had been
taken from her: she could no longer walk, go to the bathroom at her own discretion, move her right arm; she therefore was no longer held responsible for making lists of
things to do or washing dishes or making phone calls to
repairmen-crooks. In fact, she'd arrived at the situation in
life she'd always secretly longed for. Anna truly didn't have
to lift a finger in order to stay alive. And since this service
didn't cost a penny, all she had to do was lean back and
enjoy it. The state paid for everything.

Anna felt a certain satisfaction that at eighty-five, paralyzed and penniless, she was finally sitting pretty. She could
summon servants at will and she didn't have to eat another
gristly bite of meat in her life. It could be said, she thought,
that the blessed arrow of the Wheel of Fortune had finally
landed upon her.

When the rat was caught, or the corpse loaded and dis-
pensed with, an aide opened the door and announced to

· · · · ·

Anna they were moving her to another room. They did this with regularity—and without explanation. They'd dump her few robes in a cart, pull her family snapshots off the wall and tuck them under her pillow, grab her personal items out of a drawer, unscrew her little TV from the table, and off they would go, a parade of sorts, a big strong Mexican fellow at each end of her bed, a girl rolling the cart, and another aide pulling along her feeding machine. Anna had to caution them not to go too fast or the tube would pull out of her stomach and where would she be then?

100   They wheeled her down one hall and up another. She scowled at all the old geezers vegetating in the halls as they gawked at her. She didn't want those dummies in their wheelchairs drawing erroneous conclusions about her, possibly assuming she was infected with some dread organism and would end up in a room with a big red star on the door. She definitely didn't want them thinking she was being moved to the Alzheimer's wing, having lost the last of her marbles. They might even think she was dead and was going to be transported to the morgue. Well—let them! Let them get good and scared. In fact, Anna closed her eyes and let her jaw go slack, to look as dead as she could. A song from childhood came to her mind:

> *Did you ever think, when the hearse went by*
> *That you would beeee . . . the next to die?*

Death! She'd give her right arm to be the next to die. Even her *left* arm, the one that still moved.

Why should she have to go to the trouble of making the acquaintance of a new roommate? How many faceless old ladies had Anna lived with already? They all looked alike, they were all useless to her, could teach her nothing, introduce her to no one, improve her circumstances not at all. Anna had made it the main rule of her life never to cultivate

. . . . .

people who were not *important*. What was the sense of
wasting your time with the poor, the stupid, the ineffectual,
the powerless, and now, here, with the deaf, the lame, the
blind, the catatonic?

When the aide wheeled her into the new room, she knew
she was already at a disadvantage. "This is Mildred
Pierce," the aide said. "Mildred, this is Anna Goldman."
Anna could see at once that Mildred had the bed by the
window, the one with the superior view of the hallway, the
one from which she could see whomever came and went
through the outside door. Mildred, it was clear, was the
owner of the room, and that meant she had the upper
hand.

Anna refused to look Mildred in the eye or even greet
her although she could see the woman was considerably
younger, probably not a day over seventy. Installed by the
window in her wheelchair, she was within arm's reach of
her own private phone which fact immediately annoyed
Anna enormously. She'd be chattering all day and Anna
would have to listen to it. Anna also noticed that the curtains over the windows were drawn shut. She took the opportunity to make a major fuss.

"I'm entitled to see outside!" she complained to the aide.
"Do I have to live here in the dark like in a grave?" She
had found in the course of her life that it was most effective
to leap to the extreme interpretation of any plight.

The west side of the nursing home looked out at a park
where high school boys played ball. Though the rooms were
at street level and set back only two feet from the sidewalk,
Anna had been assured that people passing by couldn't see
into the windows—anyone trying to peer in would see only
his own reflection. Anna observed that her new room was
positioned at the end of a long corridor, just beside the
outside door. The door (like all the doors here) was supposed to be locked at 8 p.m., but the security guard never
bothered to lock any of them. When Anna complained, the

nurses told her that no criminal would want to come into a place full of old, helpless people.

The fact was that all kinds of people came in, day and night. There was constant traffic—doctors popping in and nurses changing shifts and aides leaving and ambulances stopping, and hearses arriving. Whatever room Anna was in, a cold breeze was always hitting her on the back of the neck.

The aide pulled back the curtain. The new roommate, Mildred Pierce (what kind of name was that? It was the name of an old movie that Joan Crawford starred in, did this woman think she was some kind of a movie star?) said, "If she wants the curtains open, by all means, leave them open."

102

"Oh drop dead," Anna muttered under her breath. "Don't do me any favors."

The woman appeared not to hear Anna and actually smiled at her. It wasn't going to work—her trying to be nice. Anna would not allow it.

Mildred Pierce picked up a big paperback and opened it. *Hawaii*, the cover said. Did this woman Mildred think she was going on a vacation any time soon? Besides, Anna knew of no one in this place who had enough eyesight left to read even a billboard. Why pretend? Did she think she was impressing Anna? Anna—in fact—could impress the ears off her and anyone else in this place if she tried. All she'd have to do was state her credentials. Anna had worked for a New York state senator. Anna had flown on one of the first commercial airline flights. Anna had owned a piano autographed by Lily Pons, the opera star. Anna had had Barbra Streisand buy something from her antique store, and not only Streisand, but Zsa Zsa Gabor, John Wayne—the Duke himself. Vivien Leigh had been in to buy a picture frame. Robert De Niro had bought for his baby son an old red wooden high chair that Anna's own grand-

· · · · ·

daughter had sat in. (If only she had the high chair today, it would be worth a fortune. What did she sell it for, fifty dollars? It had been an antique even then.) She had once had a Frederic Remington painting that she sold for two hundred dollars. She had given away for a song a signed Lalique statue. If only she had held onto everything, she'd be a multimillionaire now, and wouldn't be on Medi-Cal, and could have her own private nurses, live in her own house and not have to put up with rats and dead bodies in the halls.

"I used to be someone," she wanted to tell this Mildred Pierce, but she knew it wouldn't carry any weight. They all thought they used to be someone. In the retirement home where Anna had lived for five years (what a waste, it had cost a fortune and she hardly remembered a minute of it), the old men carried around newspaper clippings of what big shots they used to be. This one said he'd owned a car dealership, another one said he'd built the Brooklyn Bridge, the next one was a famous architect—one was always trying to prove he was a bigger deal than the next. So what? They were all slumped over little men with pacemakers or colostomies who wore their waistlines pulled up to their chins with suspenders. The women, too, liked to talk about how many husbands they'd had, how many diamonds were in the vault, how their children were fancy surgeons. Many of them had photos of themselves at age twenty on their walls. Every great beauty's face was now steam-rollered by age into the same generic old lady. Anna, too, had been beautiful; men had been after her from the day she put on nylons and got on the subway to Manhattan and took a job in a legal office.

She didn't remember much of what happened yesterday, but she had perfect recall of what had happened sixty-five years ago—how she had lied to get her first job, said she'd had years of experience. And how, on her first day at work, a man came in the door and asked her for the process server. She started opening the draws of her desk—she thought it must be something like a cake server.

"Hah!" she said aloud. A rush of other memories came back: how one day she wore a white linen suit to work and bled red menstrual blood on the back of the skirt, and how her boss (the New York state senator!) wrapped his suit jacket around her waist and tied the arms in front. He did that for her, bending over her, despite her humiliation! She was touched right now, a lifetime away, as she hadn't been then. A few days after that, he invited her on a three-day business trip to upstate New York, by train. He said he needed her stenographic services. But by then she was going out with Abram, who said she could only go on the business trip on the condition that he could come along, too, and be her bodyguard. Anna had assured him he was wrong to worry, that the senator had a wife and wasn't interested in her. But Abram said he knew better, that if Anna ever had to work late typing legal contracts, she must call him and let him sit with her in the office.

Suddenly she felt a longing for Abram, though she couldn't remember his face now. He had big hands, though —she could see them quite clearly in her mind. Big, power-ful, hairy, gentle hands.

"You want a Lifesaver?" Mildred Pierce asked.

"I don't eat by mouth," Anna said.

"You could have a Lifesaver anyway, you still have sa-liva."

"How do you know what I have?"

"I see you have legs," Mildred Pierce said.

"And you don't?"

"I don't." Mildred pulled away the knitted afghan from her wheelchair and Anna saw the stumps of her legs, cut off above her knees.

For once she was speechless. What could she say? Finally she thought of something.

"What if I wanted a Lifesaver, how could I get it? I can't walk out of this bed and you can't walk over here."

. . . . .

"I can roll," Mildred Pierce said. She began rolling her wheelchair toward Anna. She held out the roll of brightly colored hard candies.

"You're going to be a pest, I can see," Anna said.

"We might as well be on speaking terms," Mildred said, "as long as we're stuck here. Though I'm hoping to get out soon."

"Who isn't?" Anna said.

Anna felt momentarily sorry for Mildred Pierce. She wondered if her legs were already buried and waiting for her. She knew of a woman who had "one foot in the grave," a gangrenous foot (amputated) that was buried in her grave and patiently awaiting the rest of her. Anna still had everything but her teeth and her appendix. She had come close to losing a toe, but the surgeons got her circulation going again by cutting out the clogged artery and putting in a plastic one. Whoever designed the universe (she didn't mean God, how could there be a God in charge of this mess?) could have arranged for things in the body to last the same amount of time and then just fail all together. One minute you'd be up and swimming the English Channel, the next you'd shut off like a light bulb that blows out. But this arrangement! A toe goes, an esophagus closes up, a hipbone crumbles, an artery in the brain gets clogged, the pancreas stops making insulin, and the legs get cut off. What kind of an education did this dummy have—whoever it was that designed the human anatomy?

When bedtime came, Mildred Pierce did an amazing thing: she wheeled herself as close to her bed as she could, and, using her arms on the armrests, she lifted herself up and swung herself back and forth, back and forth until she had enough momentum to vault into the center of her bed! Anna gasped. What if Mildred Pierce missed her target and cannonballed herself right across the room to land on top of Anna?

. . . . .

"I'm strong," Mildred confessed to Anna. "I lost my legs young. I have arms like a wrestler."

In the morning, when the phone rang, Mildred leaned out of her bed to answer it. It was a yellow Princess phone, old-fashioned, the cord black with grime. Anna noticed that she lowered her voice and whispered. So she was going to keep secrets! What kind of secrets could an old lady have? Maybe it was money she was talking about. (She knew of rich old people in the nursing home who had hidden their millions and were letting the state pay for them.) But then she heard Mildred whisper:

"I love you." Then she whispered, "I miss you, too, darling." Then she said, "I'll see you this afternoon. Yes. It can't be soon enough. I count the minutes."

Just to hear such drivel Anna felt like throwing up. What was this baloney? She decided she would have to ask for another room change. For some reason a devil of jealousy was hammering in her chest: *I'll see you this afternoon. It can't be soon enough.* What was that all about? The people living their leftover lives here didn't have *intrigues*. Didn't have *love affairs*. For all of them, that was in the distant, dead, dessicated past. What was going on? Mildred had to be pretending. Maybe she had arranged for herself to be called by one of those party numbers, where lonely people say sexy things to strangers. Anything was possible in this world; there were varieties of sickness so varied, so perverted (Anna knew this from the Oprah Winfrey show) that nothing could surprise her.

In the afternoon, Elena, the aide, came and helped Mildred put on her earrings. Anna watched as Mildred applied rouge, lipstick, perfume. Then Elena wheeled Mildred into the hall.

"Where are you taking her?" Anna heard herself plead. "Is there an activity? Can I go too?"

"She's going to see her husband!" said Elena, throwing

back her head and rolling her eyes. "He's waiting for her in the Medicare wing."

"What husband?" Anna said, choking.

But they were out the door and gone.

Late that night, after the halls were hushed, after the eleven o'clock shift had changed, when the lights were out and the call bells had stopped ringing, long after Mildred had come back from her visit and tossed her torso into the center of her bed, long after Anna's mind had continued sizzling with confusion, pain, and especially with jealousy, the outside door creaked open slowly and Anna saw two big **107** hulking boys come in. They stood in the corridor for a moment and then ducked straight into Anna's room, which was the first door nearest the street. She could see them in the glow from the hall—two ugly boys of about fifteen, wearing turned-around baseball caps and big baggy pants.

"What do you want?" Anna said hoarsely.

"Hey old lady," one of them said. "Don't say nothin' or you're dead."

From where she lay, Anna could see one of the boys open the chest of drawers opposite her bed. Her clean robes were in the top drawer, her bedpan was in the middle drawer, her soiled robes were in the bottom drawer.

"There's nothing in there anyone could use," she said. "This is a nursing home. What could you want here?"

"You got a TV, don't you?" The boy came close to her bed and put his big hand on her little five-inch TV.

"You can't take that," Anna said. "It's screwed into the table."

"Then maybe we'll take you instead," the boy said.

"Yo," the other boy said. "You're some prize."

And suddenly, one of them whipped her blankets off her and exposed her body beneath the bunched up hospital gown. She could see with horror what they saw: her slack white belly with the hole in it, the naked tube pumping its

tasteless life into her gut, and below it, the forgotten part
that was once her sex.

"Get away from me!" Anna screamed. "Help, help,
somebody help!" she screamed. But she knew the nurses
wouldn't come; if they heard a scream they'd think it was
just some old person out of her mind. It was skeleton-shift
time; if any nurses or aides were on duty, they were having
coffee, or sitting together talking in the lounge.

"We got to have *something* from you," one of the boys
said. "We came in here to get us something. What prize
you planning to give us?"

108   Anna was frozen. She clutched her heart and felt there
the ticking of her useless, burdensome life—and found it
precious. She wanted it.

"Let's see what's up here," one boy said, trying to lift
her gown over her breasts. Her paralyzed arm held her
gown down firmly on one side. One of the boys bent over
her face; she could smell the beer on his breath. And then
the cannonball hit her bed. Like a boulder shot out of a
slingshot, the torso of Mildred Pierce landed on Anna's
bed! She could feel the weight of it smashing like a wrecking
ball into those boys, spinning like a dervish, her wrestler's
arms punching out at those boys, her furious mouth cursing
those boys and hissing like a banshee at them. Anna covered her face with her good hand so she didn't get a broken
nose.

In no time, there was a commotion in the hall and the
security guard ran in with his keys and his flashlight. He
grabbed both boys by their necks and threw them down on
the floor.

When a nurse turned the lights on in the room, Mildred
bounced her torso up toward Anna and began stroking
her face. "You're okay, honey, you're fine, don't worry, I
almost killed those little bastards."

Long into the night, after the police had come and gone
and taken the boys away in the squad car, after the nurse

had put a sedative in Anna's feeding tube, after Mildred had been carried back to her bed by an aide, Anna thought about her saved life, and about how much she wanted what she still had.

"Are you sleeping, Mildred?" Anna asked.

"No, how can I sleep? I'm thinking," Mildred whispered across the space between their beds. "I can hardly believe the guts I still have in me."

"Me, too," Anna said. "Me, too."

"I wish we could live backwards," Mildred said. "Go the other way."

"Yeah," Anna said. "Then we could be college room- **109** mates."

"I never went to college."

"I never finished high school," Anna said.

A buzzer went on at the nurses' station. It buzzed through Anna's bones like warning of an electrocution to come.

"I used to push the buzzer ten times every night when I first came here," Anna confessed to Mildred over the chasm between their beds, "just to talk to someone. But an aide once told me if I bothered him again, he'd hold a pillow over my face. But all I wanted was to talk. To any-one."

"I just want to talk to my husband," Mildred said. "I just want to be with him."

"Your husband?"

"He's dying of heart failure. He's in the Medicare wing, hooked up to oxygen and a heart monitor."

"How come you two don't live in the same room?" Anna asked. "It's only right."

"We can't. The state has rules about same-sex rooms."

"The state has rules?" Anna said. "So what? You can't let that bother you. At our age we don't pay attention to rules. Maybe you can fool the state. Maybe *we* can. Think of what we did tonight! Those boys might have killed us."

. . . . .

"We *are* tough cookies," Mildred said. "Look how long you've lived already. And me—I used to live on a farm. I drove a tractor. When the red fox went for the chickens, I killed him with one shot. Little punks like them don't scare me"

"Listen," Anna said. "Tomorrow night you tell Elena to bring your husband in here. We can switch. She can put me in his bed for the night."

Mildred was silent for a minute.

"You really think we could pull it off? You really think we could risk it?"

"So what could be so bad?" Anna said. "They'll give us a demerit? You'll lose your virginity? Don't worry."

"What if they catch us?"

"What would the punishment be?" Anna asked. "Life imprisonment? They'll arrest us?"

Mildred considered this for a moment. Then she said to Anna, "You're a doll. You're a lifesaver."

"So maybe you could throw me a Lifesaver now," Anna said. "After all the excitement, my mouth is a little dry."

HEAR NO ENTREATIES, SPEAK NO CONSOLATIONS

Anna was diminished. If she thought she'd been compromised when she lived in the retirement home, she now realized that the other had been fireworks, a festival, a parade, a county fair, the "Star-Spangled Banner." This. This was . . . she didn't have the words for it. This was a hovel in a graveyard, this was the . . . paws of an animal on her back as some two-hundred-pound dumb cluck turned her from side to side every two hours. This was the supreme insane asylum as moaners and screamers sang a chorus every night of "Call the Police, Oh Momma, Momma, come and get me, I've missed the train, untie me, when are they serving me my sand?" You could hear anything here, and you did. You could scream anything and no one cared. You could be slumped over in your wheelchair in the hall and beg a passer-by to call the police and get you out of here—and no one would help. You could tell them you were being held here against your will, that you had plenty of money to pay a lawyer, that you wanted to go home, that you could afford to hire round-the-clock private nurses, and they'd pass you by, nice-looking, decent people, here to visit their screaming mamas and papas, but as soon as they entered this charnel house, they were in a special hell whose sign above the entrance specified: *Hear No Entreaties, See No Atrocities, Speak No Consolations.*

Anna had seen her own daughters do it (to her satisfaction): pass right by some babbling crone who was slipping down out of her restraints (whose chin was snagged on the straps of her wheelchair), pass right by without so much as a glance as she begged and pleaded. Why should they help anyone here, anyway? If her daughters were coming to see *her*, they shouldn't waste one second on some crazy old coot whose mind was in Minnesota and who had one foot in the grave.

Anna was shackled: straps and ropes and chains and tubes entrapped and surrounded her; Houdini couldn't have got out of this place. Two cords (which since her stroke she couldn't pull) were for the light switch and the call-buzzer. There was a silver chain that attached and locked her five-inch TV to the bed table (otherwise it would be stolen in five minutes). On her wrists were plastic bracelets, in various neon colors, identifying her, her medications, her doctor, her room number, and one bright red bracelet blazing out "Do Not Resuscitate!" There was no chance she'd have the good luck to have her heart stop; the bracelet might as well have read "Miss America 1993" or "Lottery Winner, Five Million Dollar Jackpot." In fact, Anna could see no way that she could possibly die. She couldn't fall (her hand was paralyzed and had no strength, her hip was broken and she couldn't walk), she couldn't starve or even choke to death since she no longer ate anything by mouth, but was on a feeding tube that pumped "Gevity" (a milkshake-thick potion of enzymes and vitamins designed to threaten her with eternal longevity) into a hole in her belly, she couldn't take poison (nothing was in reach of her two working fingers but the On/Off button of the TV next to her bed), she couldn't depart this world via pneumonia, the supposed friend of the aged (since the minute she coughed they'd start pumping antibiotics into her feeding tube—and besides, she'd had the pneumonia vaccine injected into her), she had no history in her family of cancer or cirrhosis of the liver, and she never had smoked or taken a drink. Clearly this was going to be one deadly long last chapter.

112

. . . . .

"So what do you do all day, Ma?" her daughter Janet
asked during one of her many obligatory visits in the second year of Anna's incarceration, "Do you just sit there
with your mind blank?"

"I'm never blank!" Anna snapped. "Never."

"What do you think about?"

Anna stared at her daughter; how do you tell a child who
is still running to Las Vegas for vacations, still redecorating
her home, still looking forward to her daughters' weddings,
still dyeing her hair, that there were things to think about
that no one could dream could *ever* be thought about? How
much truth was a mother allowed to reveal to a child, even
if the child were fifty-five and the mother eighty-five? How
much protecting was there left to be done?

113

"I think about Daddy," Anna said. That was neutral; it
could be taken as a sentimental, reverential reflection. She
saw her daughter breathe with relief. The fact was Anna
hardly remembered him.

"I think about him, too," Janet said. (She had her purse
in her lap, clutched in her fingers, as if she wanted to leave
as soon as possible.) "He was a wonderful father," she
added, smiling at Anna to reassure her that no mistake had
been made in Anna's choice of a husband. "He was always
so full of life, he enjoyed things so much, he had such an
appetite for living!"

Anna screwed her lips shut. This wasn't the track she
was on, she wasn't going to accommodate to this. Her
mouth was dry as old corn flakes. (She was entitled to a
spearmint-flavored swab if she wanted it; the nurse would
jiggle it around on Anna's tongue if she complained loudly
enough, but she didn't want even that, hadn't swallowed
anything, food, water, even sucked on a Lifesaver, for more
than a year now.)

"Oh, he was such a good father," Janet went on. "He
would have done anything for the family, for his children
. . . He often said how much he loved us . . ."

Impatiently, Anna cut her off. "I just want to be in the

grave next to him!'' There, it had burst forth despite her pledge to herself that she would tone it down for this visit. Her daughters often left her bedside in tears, and Anna occasionally felt the slightest pang of guilt about how far she pushed them. But these outbursts were her pleasure, and she couldn't deny herself, even in the interest of sparing her children. *"That's* what I think of in my blank mind, since you want to know! I think of that space next to him, that blank space in the Jewish cemetery, right next to where he's laid out. I want my coffin, I want my peace, I want to be in it. NOW!''

114   Janet got a scared look on her face—her daughter was not young any more, she was getting heavy around the hips, she had already given up her womb and her gall bladder to the surgeon's knife. *My God,* Anna thought, *one day my darling baby is going to be tied up in one of these torture chambers, too.*

On TV, she had seen a computer-artist change a woman's face from age eighteen to age eighty-eight in a series of quick overlays. She stared at her daughter's face and repeated the process privately, lengthening her daughter's nose and chin and bringing them toward each other, creating wrinkles, bags under her eyes, dewlaps, jowls, turkey neck, long hanging earlobes, liver spots; finally she removed her daughter's teeth and let the mouth that had nursed from Anna's breast undulate and pulse like an octopus. She was transfixed by her own projection, but her daughter was chattering on, unaware of what lay ahead for her.

The curtain, which had been drawn shut between Anna's bed and The Crab's bed, billowed slightly with movement on the other side. Anna knew exactly what the old witch was up to, clacking the beads of her rosary, rolling around the room in her wheelchair to look at one sickly picture of Jesus after another that decorated the walls on her side of the room. Her daughter would be in here any minute,

．．．．．

Christmas trees hanging from her ears. The woman must
think she was an interior decorator, bringing in paper tur-
keys to glue on the wall for her mother in November, elabo-
rate crèches in December, red Valentine hearts in
February, green shamrocks and leprechauns in March, yellow Easter baskets in April. The rest of the time, when she
visited, she leaned head-to-head with The Crab as they
listened to soap operas and reruns of westerns turned to
top volume. Deaf as Anna's roommate professed to be, she
could hear like a lioness the instant Anna hummed her
private aria, her prayer, her wish, her command, her passionate entreaty: "I wish I were dead."

"You spoil my digestion when you say that," The Crab
complained to her the minute a nurse pulled the curtain
back. "It's bad for my appetite and makes me feel as if I'm
in a mental institution."

An appetite? Anyone who had an appetite here *belonged*
in a mental institution. Before Anna had had her stroke,
she was forced to partake of the food they served on this
toothless wing: green slime for salad, brown mush for
steak, red and yellow ribbons of Jell-O, pink liquefied
syrup they called cake.

"To think," Anna said to her daughter now, "that people want to live to a great old age. They should have their
heads examined."

"Would you rather have died young like Daddy?" her
daughter challenged her. "Dead from leukemia at fifty-
five? Never to live to enjoy his grandchildren? Or see the
world change the way you have?"

"So he didn't get to see a microwave," Anna said. "But
think how lucky he was that he never got old. Am *I* lucky—
to see every power taken away, piece by piece, till nothing is
left? Look at me. I used to play the piano, I used to walk, I
used to eat, I used to smile. Now I'm a piece of meat, they
turn me over like a roast, they poke things into me, I'm an

open village, anyone can come into my private roads.'' She saw her daughter throw a look of exasperation at the ceiling. Anna looked, too. What were those reddish spots up there—blood? Had someone's high blood pressure, once-upon-a-time, burst through the top of her head and shot a geyser up to the ceiling? Was that someone's lucky stroke out of here?

''If only you had a better attitude, Mom,'' her daughter began. ''Other people in here, after a few months, accept their situation, they don't carry on like you do, they recognize that when a person lives this long, this is the price you pay; when you get to be very old, your body finally wears out. At least be grateful your mind hasn't worn out; you know everything that goes on, you're as sharp as ever.''

''That's my problem. I'd be better off a vegetable. I could babble all night and think I was a flying cow.''

''But Ma—after two years here, can't you at least try to accept . . . ?''

Accept? Accept? What was she talking about? Anna didn't want a sermon. She already got sermons from the nurses, who told her she made too much fuss about every little thing, sermons from The Crab, who didn't approve of her death wish and told she had to wait until The Good Lord called, sermons from the aides who soaked her gown every time they injected medicine into her feeding tube and then blamed her for letting the tube clog up.

The Orthodox Jew who owned the place marched into her room (and the rooms of the two or three other Jewish residents) on High Holy Days, holding up a ragged piece of matzo or a couple of Chanukah candles and giving sermons about ''Our Heritage,'' and ''Our Magnificent History.'' He was maybe twenty-five, with a beard like an octogenarian, and hard little black eyes. What did he know of heritage and history? Anna could see he hadn't lived life at all; he was a small-minded, tough, mean businessman, making babies with his orthodox wife who wore a babushka like

116

from the old country. Anna knew he sat in his office all day peering at charts on his computer and schemed ways to have the nursing home make more money. He watered down the prune juice, he served horse-meat, he refused Anna her disposable diapers.

Even her daughters didn't know about the diapers—what the nursing home did to Anna after she came back from her second surgery. (The first—she reminded herself —was to get the circulation going in her leg so they wouldn't have to cut off her rotting toe; the second was after her stroke, when she tried to get out of bed in the hospital and broke her hip. Why they'd bothered to re-place her hip she didn't know. She hadn't walked a step since.)

It was then, upon her return to the nursing home, that the aides starting using diapers. They claimed it was easier than having to run when she called for a bedpan every ten seconds, easier than hearing her complain of pain when they hoisted her on it, then complain again when they left her on it too long before they came back to take it away. So Anna got diapers. What did she care? She knew the seven ages of man. Why should she be different? Like Methu-selah, like anyone who lived past eighty, she was becoming an infant without teeth, a baby who peed in bed, who couldn't walk, who couldn't turn over herself, a baby who was going backward into the sea of time till soon she'd sink under, her head disappearing, and be gone. (But not soon enough!)

When Medicare stopped paying for the diapers after a hundred days, the Orthodox Jew and his henchman came in and told Anna they'd have to call her daughters and report that her time on Medicare was up. If her family wanted diapers for her, they'd have to pay fifty dollars a box for them.

"Not on your life," Anna had told the men (who looked to her like Tweedle Dee and Tweedle Dum with beards). "I won't have my children wasting a penny on me. If your aides weren't so lazy, if they were willing to bring me a bed pan, if they treated me like a human being, I wouldn't be in diapers to begin with. So now you figure it out. It doesn't matter to me if I don't have diapers. I'll just wet the bed."

The men stepped into the hall to hold a feverish consultation. They argued in great agitation as if over a point of law in the Torah—this pettiness was in their genes. Also, they had seen Anna carry on and knew she wasn't bluffing.

The solution they reached was a device now in place between her legs—some kind of thick rag (supplied by the nursing home) which, at intervals, was pulled out by an aide and replaced with a new one.

No, there were tortures in this existence her daughters had not yet begun to imagine: the bowel impactions, for example, which had happened to Anna several times due to her inactivity and her lack of solid food. When this occurred, when the aides noted that a week had passed without results, they set upon her some young Mexican aide (sometimes a young fellow just over the border and working cheap) who was given license by the nurses (who hated to do it themselves) to thrust his gloved fingers into Anna's private recesses to unstick the stalled products of digested "Gevity." She had to submit. She had no choice. She sometimes screamed in pain during the procedure. And in recent weeks she imagined the worst, that maybe one certain aide enjoyed doing it to her, came in during the dark hours after midnight and turned her on her side, did things to her behind her back, said it was orders on her chart from the doctor. He took a long time doing it, with her turned on her side, away from him. She couldn't see his face or tell exactly what he was doing (and maybe not doing things only to her). She didn't know his name. She didn't even know if he worked here. Who would believe her if she told anyone her fears? And if she reported him and he was fired, who knew what he would do, come back with a gun and kill her?

Kill her children! Never mind. What did it matter? She wasn't a woman. She was no longer human, no longer a sexual being.

When her turn came to be showered here, by male aides or female aides, it was all the same, they sat her naked on a chair with a hole in it, wheeled her under the cascading blasts of water—first too cold, then too hot. They used a washcloth first on her body, her private parts, and then, last of all . . . on her face. She was outraged; she sat there, freezing, burning, singing her tune, "I wish I were dead," saying it out loud and to herself, shouting it, like a Hallelujah chorus, filling her mouth with water and spitting out the words.

So how did her daughter have the nerve to tell her she should have a better attitude?

Her attitude had worsened after she had learned the cost of her hospital bill from her hip surgery. She still couldn't believe it. *Eighty-seven thousand dollars!* For consultations and tests and machines and technicians and therapists and surgeons and heart specialists and lung specialists and blood specialists and brain specialists and stomach specialists and several psychiatrists to find out why she wanted to die. (Their brilliant diagnosis was: "Depression possibly related to recent health setbacks.") All this knowledge for Anna's benefit, all these geniuses gathered around her singing gibberish:

> *There was an old lady who fell out of bed,*
> *We can't make her well,*
> *We can't make her dead.*

No wonder Medicare had no money left for her diapers. But what bothered her was the stupidity of it. Eighty-seven thousand dollars? Anna had never seen that much money in her life, not at one time, not in one place. But to think what money like that would have bought her at another

．．．．．

time of her life, another place. An education! Music lessons with a master teacher. A house for herself and her husband and children. Freedom, space, the ocean, the mountains, rivers, eagles flying overhead. Maybe even vacations (which she and Abram could never afford to take), a night in a hotel, good meals in restaurants, a car that wasn't fifteen years old. She couldn't bear to think about this; the tube in her stomach, the machine pumping in the "Gevity"—this alone cost eight hundred dollars a month, more than Anna had ever paid for rent, ever, anywhere, in all the places she had lived in her life. For the conveniences she had now, a narrow bed, a five-inch TV, and all the complimentary tortures of this existence, someone was writing a check for thousands of dollars every month to the Orthodox Jew with his beard and his matzo crumbs.

"How can I get in touch with Dr. Death?" Anna asked her daughter. "This Kevorkian doctor. I want to speak to him."

"He would never consider you, Ma," her daughter said. "You're not terminally ill. You're not even dying."

"What would you call this?" Anna asked.

"That's not the point. You don't have a fatal condition."

"I have the human condition."

"Yes, but you're not *dying. Not right now.*"

"Excuse me," Anna said. "Are you suggesting I'm dancing the night away?"

"You make it hard for me, Ma. I don't know what to say. If I could fix you, I would. I'd do anything if I could. But I'm only human, too." Her daughter looked over toward The Crab's side of the room; Anna knew what she was thinking. When The Crab's daughter visited, the two of them chatted briefly, played three hands of gin rummy, prayed to Jesus, watched TV, and then said a brisk goodbye. No operatic crescendos, no Sarah Bernhardt pronouncements, no farewell deathbed scenes. But The Crab didn't have Anna's grasp of the nature of existence. She didn't see the long view and therefore couldn't make judgments. She didn't excoriate the universe; she simply didn't have the brains for it.

"Janet, have a little human sympathy for me." (She knew she should leave it alone, but she couldn't.) "I have nothing to do here all day but think of how I'm in pain, how I'm suffering. How they turn me over every two hours. How I have a bed sore at the base of my spine. How my right arm is swollen and paralyzed. How my heels hurt. How I have a pain in my chest all the time."

"Ma, maybe if you thought of something else besides yourself. I always offer to bring you books on tape and a cassette player. You could listen to all the great books you never read. You could finally get your education!"

"I'm not interested. What do I need an education for now? To help me in my future career?"

"To enlarge your horizons. You could listen to tapes of all the music you love. For pleasure. Beethoven, Chopin, Mozart."

"Just thinking of a piano makes my heart break. Hearing one would kill me."

"So it would kill you. I thought that's what you want, anyway," Janet said. "Look, I'm sorry, Ma. I didn't mean that. But what is, is. This is where you are. This is your fate now. You have to make the best of it."

"Give me liberty or give me death," Anna said.

"If I actually handed you a poison pill, would you take it right now?" her daughter demanded. For an instant, Anna thought her daughter was going to produce one from her pocket.

"You know I can't swallow anything by mouth," Anna said in self-defense. "I'm on a feeding tube."

Anna checked the large-print schedule taped to the wall and saw that there was an "activity" taking place in Unit Nine. She was getting bored by her own histrionics.

"You'll wheel me over, I'll enlarge my horizons," she

．．．．．

told her daughter. "They drag in all these unconscious souls who sleep and drool the whole time, while some poor girl from Mexico, who can hardly speak English, asks us if anyone knows how much two-plus-two is, and then she reads us recipes from the paper for chili beans. Tell me, Janet, are any of us going to be cooking chili beans in the near future?" Anna motioned with her movable fingers to her daughter. "Go get the nurse now and tell her to unhook me from the feeding tube. It's pumping me so full that I'm gaining five pounds a week. I never weighed more than 105 in my life and now I'm 133 pounds. Tell the nurse I want to be put into the wheelchair."

Anna braced herself for the ordeal. Two male aides came in and, chattering to each other in Spanish as if Anna were not there at all, they rolled and jerked her around on her bed. First they needed to put on Anna's cotton robe. They needed to change the wet diaper-rag. They needed to undo the feeding tube from its socket and insert the sealer plug. Anna's daughter waited discreetly in the hall while they got her dressed and lifted her into the padded wheelchair. Anna screamed repeatedly as they pinched her skin, hoisted her roughly, dropped her down too hard, nearly broke her ribs as they let go of her. When her daughter finally wheeled her down the corridor past the reflecting window of the beauty parlor, Anna turned away her head. "I haven't looked at myself in a mirror since I've been here. Why would I want to look at a corpse?"

"Jesus loves me, this I know, for the Bible tells me so."
The song coming from the activity room hit Anna like a hot wind. "I forgot. Bible Study is on Thursday," she told Janet. "Turn me around." They were in the breezeway between units; the goldfish fountain gurgled and sloshed gum wrappers among the mottled, bloated-looking fish. White-coated aides, the beautiful dark-haired young men and women on their breaks, sat on the hard metal chairs and flirted, teased, laughed, as if this place they worked in

were a carnival, a celebration on the outskirts of town where the freaks were incidental, where the true purpose of their work was pleasure, laughter, and seduction. They had shining skin, ebony hair, brilliant smiles; they were aching to start making their thousands of babies together, Anna could feel the urgency in their voices.

Janet had stalled the wheelchair; Anna didn't really want to go back to her room and stare at The Crab, not after all her arduous preparations, repositionings, and mechanical adjustments, nor did she especially want to hear that Jesus loved her. Clapping could be heard from the activity room; a man's deep voice exhorted everyone to join in.

"Oh, wheel me in, anyway," Anna conceded. "What can we lose?" Janet turned her in a circle and pushed on. Inside it looked like a train station full of the lame and the halt waiting for passage to Lourdes. Anna wondered how it would be now if she'd been raised a believer. Jesus up on a cloud, arms extended, to welcome her into heavenly bliss, Jesus to forgive her meanness and sarcasm, Jesus happy to bathe her brow in the waters of peace. Jesus her handsome lover there to soothe her pains, console her for her losses, cherish her tenderly for eternity.

Instead, what legacy did she have from her own pale religious beginnings? Nothing but the memory of a father who forbade her to sing the name of Jesus in Christmas carols at the public school. And now what did she have? An Orthodox Jew-businessman with a long beard waving matzos at her.

Janet bumped her over the threshold and found a place for Anna under a vent that already was blowing cold air on her neck and would probably give her pneumonia that wouldn't kill her. Janet herself took a seat on a torn plastic couch beside a Down's Syndrome woman (she could have been fifteen years old or thirty) wearing a pink apron with bunnies on it.

Anna scrutinized the crowd; she didn't recognize a single

person. These inmates were *young*—they had to be from
some other circle of hell, not the toothless wing or the
Alzheimer's wing. The young man conducting Bible Study,
the one with the deep voice, was very tall, very handsome.
He wore tight blue jeans with a silver belt buckle, and a
plaid shirt open at the neck with a bolo tie hanging loose
on his hairy chest. He was talking now in deep, low tones
that resonated right up through the wheels of Anna's chair
and shivered into her lacelike, filigreed bones.

"Are you impatient?" he asked. "Are you tired of waiting for the miracle? Do you think it will never come?"
124 Anna looked her daughter's way and rolled her eyes. Janet
seemed to be listening attentively, without hostility. "Do
you wake up every day and think, 'Today I'll be saved?
Today I'll be released and go home to my Heavenly
Father?' "

There was a murmur of agreement in the room. Anna
glanced around again, looking to see if any of the usual
senile vegetables, the living dead, the comatose catatonics,
had been wheeled in. But around her were only the hollow-
eyed young, the MS victims, the severely retarded, the
quadriplegics, the Lou Gehrigs, the anorexics past the
point of no return. Her heart skipped a beat then landed
in her gut like an anchor thrown from a ship. (Was *this*
going to be her fatal heart attack? Here, now, with Jesus
flapping his wings overhead?)

"My wife left me years ago," the handsome man said,
"and every year, on our anniversary, I ask myself, 'Is this
the year she'll return to me?' I always set out some flowers
on the hall table, and I look out the window for her, hoping
to see her, with her beautiful gold hair, coming up the walk.
Like all of you, I'm tired of waiting. I'm full of despair.
But then one day it occurred to me: the longer I've waited,
the closer I am to the day it will happen! So you see? *We're
all closer! Every one of us. We're almost there!* Don't you
just feel it? If the miracle wasn't yesterday, isn't today—it

. . . . .

may be . . . tomorrow! Even tonight! Because it's coming, we all know that, don't we?''

A shimmer of assent, like the whirr of hummingbirds' wings, fluttered across the room. Anna felt the breeze of it lift the hair on her neck (unless what she felt was the air vent). Just in front of her was a tiny girl-like woman on a downy fluff of deep padding, in a wheelchair designed like a reclining couch. The girl was emaciated, weighed less than a bird, couldn't have been more than twenty. Her short fine hair was cut like a boy's. She was watching the handsome man with her huge, dark eyes, beautiful eyes, she was following his every movement, taking in his power, his sweetness. Anna had an impulse to call out to him, ''Never mind about your wife, come and take care of this girl, she's lonely, she needs you. Put your arms around her. Kiss her with your lips. Give her a taste of love before it's all over.''

Now Anna noticed a young man strapped upright into a wheelchair, his face newly shaven (she saw a spot of blood on his cheek, the aide must have nicked him), but he had red lips, blue eyes, he was beautiful. He, too, was listening to the handsome man who promised the coming miracle. Next to him was a wasted young man, displaying the angles of his skeleton. He looked like the AIDS victims Anna had seen on television. Perhaps he had tasted too much love and was dying of it. She saw spastics and cripples and mutes—with their faces radiant and lit from above.

''So let's sing a song of praise now,'' the handsome man said. ''We have much to be thankful for since every one of us will very soon know ultimate love in Our Father's embrace. Just hang on, brothers and sisters. These troubled days are just a lightning flash on the vast skies of eternity.''

He pushed a button and a scratchy recording came blasting out of his tape player on a card table: ''Jesus loves me, this I know . . .''

Those who could sing, joined in. Those who were unable

watched the sunbeams dance in front of their eyes and imagined their deliverance. Anna saw her horizons widen. She saw her mother and father waiting for her on a cloud in heaven, their arms outstretched. The gentle face of her husband was smiling out of the blue skies at her. He waved, with the hand wearing his horseshoe ring; his eyes were sparkling with anticipation. She could feel herself in his strong arms, feel the power of the hug he was waiting to give her.

Anna reached over toward her daughter with her two good fingers. Janet grasped her hand tightly, bending her head and kissing her mother's fingers, one by one, over and over.

"Everyone here is young," Anna whispered to her, "but I'm very old. I've lived my whole life."

"Yes, you're very old, Ma."

"I've had the whole thing," Anna said, amazed. She actually felt peace descending on her, heavily, without grace, like a pelican coming to land on a rock. "There's nothing more for me to do. I just realized, darling—I'm at the very end. I don't have to worry anymore. That's all there is to it."

126

ANNA IN CHAINS

Anna had sung her song, her mantra, her aria for the last five years to any one who would listen, to a world audience, bigger—she estimated—than the Pope himself commanded.

"Shoot me, get me a gun, bring me a poison pill! I want to be dead! I want to be in my grave! I want to die."

When the aides didn't answer her call bell, she loudly intoned the stanzas of her libretto; when her daughters visited (then went out in the hall to get something for her from the nurse), she whispered it. In the dark of night, when the other crazies up and down the hall were singing their own songs, she chimed in with her lyric: *"Dead oh dead oh give me—dead."*

"You don't mean it," her roommate, The Crab, told her. "Don't be like the boy who cried wolf."

Anna knew all about the boy who cried wolf. Like her, he had been rehearsing for the real thing, for the moment of greatest need—but no one seemed to understand that a person had to practice, had to find the right tone, the perfect modulation, the impeccable rhythm, as in any piece of music. Anna knew all about music—she was nothing if not a musician.

Besides, the reactions engendered by her litany entertained her during the endless hours of her incarceration. Just as when she used to play the old upright piano—briefly—in the chapel of the nursing home (she had only a

few weeks of being ambulatory before her stroke, before
her broken hip), and people used to wag their heads in awe
at her rendition of the "Moonlight Sonata," she now—
when she sang her tune *("Bring me cyanide, bring me
arsenic!")*—took satisfaction in watching all those about
her rushing away in alarm.

Each tender new young Mexican aide scurried to the
nurse with the desperate news: "The lady in room 615 says
she wants to die." Anna cocked her ear for the reply: "Oh
—that one. She says that all the time. Pay no attention."

"It's a sin," one young black-haired beauty repri-
manded her as she changed the wet sheets on Anna's bed.
The child, angelic of face, with dazzling black eyes, was
only eighteen and already had three babies that her mother
cared for while she worked. "You mustn't say that anymore. You have to be patient and wait till Jesus calls you."

"I don't know from Jesus," Anna said. "And I don't
want to."

News of her daring got around. All the aides at the nursing home were recent arrivals from Mexico and staunch
Catholics; all the nurses were Protestants; the owner was
an Orthodox Jew. Those who attended Anna feared she was
daring God—tempting destruction to rain down upon all
of them. An earthquake might strike, a fire might rage
through the nursing home. What did Anna care? She'd
take death any way it came, the sooner the better. Besides,
she didn't believe anyone was up there listening to her
dares. She had once seen her suicidal son-in-law fling a can
of beer up into the branches of a tree, screaming, "Fuck
you, God!"—and *that* she had to admit was going a little
too far. But the poor demented man was dead now, and
God had had nothing to do with it. Her daughter's husband
had done himself in with means Anna could never find the
strength or technical ability to execute.

She reflected on the suicides that had passed through her
history. In 1933, a first cousin of hers named Bertha had

secretly married an Italian bartender. For the first year, too ashamed to tell her family she'd done the forbidden thing and married a non-Jew, she lived at home with her parents and only met him once a week, in the back room of the bar where he worked, to have sex with him in the storeroom among the liquor bottles. When one day Bertha's mother discovered a wedding band hidden in her daughter's box of sanitary napkins, she locked Bertha out of the house. After the young bride had moved in with her Italian husband, it turned out he found Bertha too dull and demure for his loud family gatherings. One Sunday morning—as the story went—he told her he didn't want her coming to his brother's wedding, he would have more fun without her. As soon as he left the house, she stuffed towels in the cracks under all the doorways, put the cat out, and turned on the gas.

Gert, Anna's younger sister, told the story repeatedly as a cautionary tale, as a warning against intermarriage, and as purely ghoulish gossip. In fact, Gert had always had a fascination with suicide. She often recounted the story of her best friend, Tessie, who was in love with a dentist. The dentist had given Tessie an engagement ring and convinced her "to go all the way" before their marriage. But he broke the engagement when he fell in love with one of his patients. (Gert relished adding: "And this 'patient' had a bust bigger than Jane Russell's. Men are animals, they can't control themselves.") Tessie, as Gert told the story, climbed up onto his fire escape one night, knocked on his window, and slit her wrists. The dentist wasn't even home—all Tessie's efforts were for naught. The dentist, putting out some buttermilk to cool on the fire escape the next morning, found her there, dead, with her blouse open and a suicide note in her brassiere.

Gert had always kept a little Swee Touch Nee tin tea box in her handkerchief drawer filled with yellowed newspaper clippings about suicides. Anna thought about her sister, now rich as a queen, having buried two husbands, the last one of whom had squirreled away half a million dollars. He'd bought Lane Bryant stock in its early days, correctly predicting that women would keep getting bigger and fatter and would keep buying Lane Bryant clothes. Gert lived now in a fancy Beverly Hills retirement home, from which she never stirred to come and visit Anna. Anna's daughters pled excuses for Gert: the hour's ride was too much for her, she suffered from arthritis, she soon needed cataract surgery, she had to stay near her bathroom because her bladder was so weak.

130   Anna was not impressed. Her sister, always busy doing good work for Jewish causes (for which she always got medals and plaques at donor dinners to hang on the walls all over her apartment), didn't have the kindness of heart to come and visit her helpless, paralyzed, invalid sister. To do a "mitzvah" for her own flesh-and-blood was beyond her goodness of heart.

The truth had been evident from their childhood on— Gert had always been jealous of Anna. She had always wanted everything Anna ever had—including Anna's husband and Anna's daughters. Luckily for Anna, there wasn't a single thing about Gert that Anna had ever envied.

One rainy afternoon, after the nurse had pumped the afternoon medications into Anna's feeding tube (she could feel the pulverized pills, diluted by water, rise up cold and sour into her throat as the nurse shot them into the tube with a fat syringe), a tall, unshaven, toothless old man, wearing a bathrobe and blue nursing-home slippers, padded into Anna's room. He was carrying a Bible. His skinny wrist was decorated with colorful plastic bracelets including a red one (like one Anna wore) indicating "Do Not Resuscitate!"

"I understand there's a woman in here who keeps saying she wants to die," he announced. "Is that you?" he demanded, sticking his grizzly face a foot away from Anna's.

. . . . .

"What's it to you?" she said.

"I came to save you," he said, brandishing the Bible. "You won't want to die if you accept the Lord."

"*Beethoven* is my lord," Anna said. She gestured toward the plastic bust of Beethoven she kept on her side table, the only decoration she permitted, whereas her roommate had junk everywhere—fake flowers, stuffed bunnies, crucifixes, leprechauns.

"Him! That deaf German? He can't give you everlasting life, Lady. Do you know Satan hears your wishes? He's going to *have* you if you're not careful."

"So let him have me," Anna said. "I'm no bargain."

"Do you ever think about the devil?" the old man demanded.

"No," Anna said. "Never."

"Well, *he thinks about you.*"

"Oh, go away. I ought to know what I want to think about," Anna said fiercely. "I'm eighty-eight years old, as old as there are keys on a piano."

"You could be saved! You should find the Lord!" the man said, wild-eyed, beginning to back out of the room.

"Is he so stupid that he's *lost?*" Anna yelled after him. "Just stay out of here, you lunatic. You . . . nothing. You . . . no one!"

"Are you my children?" Anna said to her daughters when they next visited her.

Anna's daughters exchanged a glance. "Yes, we're your children, Ma," they both said at the same moment. They pulled the two pink plastic chairs allotted to visitors closer to her bed.

"My memory is losing me," Anna said. "What did my husband die of? What did he look like?" She really couldn't remember. "Do you girls have any children?"

Her daughters began their patient, extended explanations. One had three daughters, one had two sons, one of the sons had two babies, a boy and a girl—the names swirled around Anna's head. These descendants of hers meant nothing to her—did they ever come and visit? She let her daughters talk and took none of it in; while they set the record straight she would have a little time to rest and think about what pleased her.

On the other side of the curtain, Anna's roommate, The Crab, mumbled, "blah blah blah." She hated when Anna's daughters visited, because apparently they all talked too much for her taste. So what? The Crab always had a rosary in her hands—let her commune with the Lord if she felt neglected.

132   After a while Anna said, "That's enough about family trees. What else can you tell me?"

Her daughters exchanged another glance. This time an alarm went off in Anna's head. She caught something in their look—they were keeping something from her.

"What is it?" she demanded. "What happened? Are one of you sick?" Her girls were no spring chickens. If one of them had cancer, Anna would kill herself! Under no circumstances did she intend to outlive her children.

"It's about Aunt Gert," her older daughter said finally.

"What about her?"

"She's been very depressed lately," her younger daughter said.

"What could she have to be depressed about!" Anna demanded. "She lives in some fancy Beverly Hills place where they take them on tours to see movie stars' houses and the shark from *Jaws*."

"She's old, Ma. She lonely, she's widowed, like you. She's sick, her back hurts, she's going deaf, her eyes are failing."

"So? I can't walk! I can't eat! I'm paralyzed. I'll never play the piano again. Do you see me being depressed?"

"Never mind. Maybe we shouldn't talk about this."

"Let's talk about it. So what else about Gert?" Anna felt a sense of alarm that Gert was about to gain some critical advantage over her.

. . . . .

"Well, the truth is, we think she tried to kill herself."

"How, by eating pork?" Anna asked.

Her daughters were silent.

Anna had to think about this. Finally she said, "Is she dead?"

"No. It seems she took too many sleeping pills. When she didn't come down for breakfast, they sent someone up to her room, and found her there."

"So what happens now? She's not going to *live* with one of you girls, is she?"

"No, but the fact is we'll have to visit her more often, keep a close eye on her."

"I wouldn't bother if I were you," Anna said. "All she wants is attention."

Anna's daughters exchanged the "Let's get going look." She saw them both stand up at once.

"Okay, Ma. We'll be back to see you soon."

"Gert should have had children of her own if she was going to need so much attention. I hope she knows she isn't going to get it from *my* children."

"Don't worry. We know we belong to you. You never let us forget it."

All night Anna was distraught. She hadn't felt this worried in a long time. Gert, even without an Italian husband, without a dentist or a fire escape, had almost accomplished what Anna most longed for—oblivion. Now Gert would probably have a fancy psychiatrist (a luxury Anna had never had in her entire life), and the next time she took too many pills they'd take her to that hospital in Beverly Hills where all the movie stars went—George Burns, Elizabeth Taylor. This was not acceptable.

Anna considered her options. Even if she had pills, she couldn't take them by mouth. She would need a mortar and pestle to grind them up and then would have to bribe someone to shoot the mixture into her feeding tube. If she had a gun, even if she knew how to use one, she was right-handed and her right hand was paralyzed. What were the words of that Dorothy Parker poem? Anna had memorized it in her youth—about how razors pain you, rivers are damp, acids stain you, drugs cause cramp—and the rest of it, gas smells bad, nooses give, guns aren't lawful, you might as well live. Dorothy Parker was only playing with words—she'd had something to live for, all that fame and money, till she drank herself to death. If Anna had some Manischewitz wine here, she would gulp the whole bottle down at once. (She could still *use* her mouth, she could still swallow. She simply chose not to, she let the feeding tube do all the work.)

134

The tube, then, was the only way she could kill herself. The "Gevity" that slithered day and night into her guts had to be cut off, stopped. If her sister Gert had the guts to take sleeping pills, Anna could at least starve herself. There were two ways to do it—stop the machine from pumping, or pull out the tube itself. Could she do either one?

For days and nights, Anna pondered this subject. She organized her thoughts; she hadn't been a legal secretary for nothing. She knew how to reason, she was simply waiting for the moment to act. On shower days, which were Tuesday and Saturday, the aide always turned off the feeding tube pump and unplugged the feeding tube from the segment implanted in Anna's belly in order to wheel Anna into the shower room. Once or twice, after she returned Anna to her bed, she forgot—in her hurry to get to the lunch room and have her enchiladas—to restart the pump. But eventually the nurse or the aide discovered the error and corrected it. Besides, Anna had heard that starving to death could take a month or more. That did not actually appeal to her very much. She had always been an impatient person, and she liked immediate results. However, if that was her only option, she could deal with it. She was sure

· · · · ·

the appropriate opportunity would present itself—she simply had to be alert enough to seize the moment when it arrived the way the wolf, in the ancient story, finally seized the boy.

On a Monday when Anna had already been disconnected from her feeding tube and hoisted into her wheelchair, waiting to be taken to the scale to be weighed—which was the monthly ritual here—the old guy in the blue slippers came back, peered into her room, and guffawed. "Hah, Lady—I see you're still alive, whether you want to be or not."

Anna knew the moment was upon her.

"Oh hello again," she said. "How nice to see you. What's your name, by the way?" she asked sweetly.

"Ludwig," he said.

"So you remember our talk?"

"What talk?"

"I wonder if you would wheel me down to the chapel."

"You want to pray?"

"I've had a lot of time to think. I've come around to a whole new way of seeing things."

"I think you should wait till Sunday when they have a priest here to say Mass. He does the whole business."

"No, I want to go now. I have no time to lose."

"I have more time than money, myself." The old man shuffled into the room, unlocked the brake of Anna's wheelchair, and began pushing her down the hall. She didn't like the way he was driving—maybe he was drunk, he reminded her of a drunk, with the stubble on his face, without all his teeth—but his driving record wasn't foremost in her mind. He was pushing her so fast she felt the wind on her face. Wildly they sped past the nursing station, past the shower rooms, past the activity room—she hadn't been on a trip like this since the roller-coaster in Coney Island.

. . . . .

He pushed open the door of the chapel. Two skinny stained-glass windows threw green light into the room on either side of a wooden cross. In the corner, just as she remembered it, was the upright piano.

"Could you leave me right there?" Anna asked. "In front of the piano?"

"I'll wait while you pray," he said. "Otherwise, you could be left here till Sunday."

"Don't worry," Anna said. "You go on ahead. I'll be fine. Just push me in a little bit closer to the keys, maybe I can play a hymn."

It was that easy. He probably didn't want to sit around while she played hymns. He just left her there—he didn't even preach to her. He had probably already forgotten why he'd come, one of the benefits of senile dementia.

In the muffled silence of the chapel, Anna bowed her head over the keys. The greenish light descending in long rays upon the keyboard was full of sun-lit dust motes. With enormous effort Anna lifted her left hand from her lap and laid it on the keys. She remembered a song from her childhood songbook, and began to hum it:

> *Seated one day at the organ,*
> *I was weary and ill at ease . . .*
> *And my fingers wandered idly*
> *Over the noisy keys . . .*

Anna tried to play a chord but her shaky fingers had no strength in them and collapsed on the discolored ivories without calling forth even one clear note.

"It doesn't matter," she said aloud. "I didn't come here to play at Carnegie Hall." Using all her strength, she wrenched her buttocks from the seat of the wheelchair and tumbled to the floor. She began to roll. She had had much practice in rolling, the aides rolled her from side to side every two hours, day and night, in her bed to keep her from getting bedsores.

Anna rolled herself around to the far side of the piano— it took her an hour or two to cover the distance—and succeeded in wedging herself in the space between the back of the piano and the wall. That was all. Now she would die here, unobserved, slowly departing life in the shadow of the great instrument that she loved, the piano that was the passion of her life. She would die heroically, suffering as Beethoven suffered, and thus doing she would accomplish all her goals, mainly beating her sister Gert to suicide, and finally dying and getting out of this place.

Anna woke in chains. She was bound, hand and foot, to the rails of her bed. She seemed also to be in some kind of a straitjacket—she couldn't tell exactly. The feeding tube was humming away beside her, she was clearly alive and in business again.

"Get me a doctor!" she screamed, and was surprised at the fierceness in her voice. She had never called for a doctor in the past, she had only called for death. Perhaps she had suffered brain damage, being stuck behind the piano for so long. "A doctor! A doctor! Get me a doctor!"

At some point in the day, a handsome bearded fellow materialized beside her bed. He looked like Abram, her dead husband, when he was young. His eyes were greenish-blue and had a Jewish sweetness in their gaze. The boy— he couldn't be more than thirty—pulled up a chair and took Anna's paralyzed hand tenderly in his own.

"Hello, Anna. I'm Dr. Arthur Kramer. I'm a psychiatrist and I've been called in to help you. My plan—with your permission—is to visit you often from now on with the goal of getting you back to a place where you can enjoy life again."

"Would you really call this 'life'?" Anna demanded. "Tell me the truth, Doctor. I know you're a smart boy, a dummy doesn't go so many years to medical school. Is this condition I have what you'd call 'life'?''

Anna indicated her shackles. She rattled the bed rails with what little strength she had in her good hand. Something about the vulnerability in the boy's face suggested she could take liberties with him. He looked a little frightened, in fact. She might even be his first geriatric patient.

"It *is* your life, whatever you call it, Anna. It's what you've got."

"So who needs it? Would *you* want it?"

"I don't think we should talk about me, Anna. We're **138** here to talk about you. We're going to do a lot of talking, and I'm going to start you on some medicine that may help you adjust."

"Adjust to what?"

"The many losses you have suffered, the losses we *all* suffer as we age. My job is to teach you how to grieve your losses."

"Maybe you should find another job then," Anna said. "I don't need a teacher for suffering. I'm already an expert in the field."

"Maybe you'll see it differently after a while. Perhaps in time you will, with the wisdom your years have given you, be willing to take on the new challenges of great old age and try to conquer them."

"Do you always talk this way?" Anna said, "because though you're a very nice boy, I don't have much patience."

The doctor was looking down; Anna had a sense that he might have choked up, even have tears in his eyes. She wanted to take him in her arms and assure him that her torment wasn't really as bad as it looked to him, that she liked to exaggerate for effect. On a good day she could even consider this life of hers an adventure.

"What's the matter, Arthur? You have a grandma about my age?"

· · · · ·

He raised his head. "Will you work with me, Anna? I'll try to be brief when I explain things to you."

"Tell me something. You're married? You have children?" Anna asked.

"I have a wife, yes, and a son, a little boy," the doctor said.

"I understand. You have to earn a living," Anna agreed. "Look, so I'll cooperate, Medicare will pay you. I'll let you come and keep me company and talk till your half-hour or whatever is up. But you should know I don't really believe in this psychology baloney. You talk but I don't have to listen. I'll ignore you, which is exactly what I do when my daughters come to see me. But I want you to understand, Arthur-the-psychiatrist: there's nothing you can teach me about life. I've lived three times as long as you have. So if I'm not paying attention, you'll be kind enough not to force yourself on me. Maybe I'll be thinking about how I danced with Abram at my wedding, how the gardenias he gave me smelled like the entire Brooklyn Botanical Gardens in springtime, how the edges of the corsage were already turning brown when we got to Atlantic City for our honeymoon. You can rest assured—I have enough to think about till the end of time."